SAINT THOMAS MORE OF LONDON

Saint Thomas More of London

Written by Elizabeth M. Ince

ILLUSTRATED BY LILI RÉTHI

A Vision Book

IGNATIUS PRESS   SAN FRANCISCO

Cover art by Christopher J. Pelicano
Cover design by Riz Boncan Marsella

Published in 2003 by Ignatius Press, San Francisco
Published by arrangement with
Farrar, Straus and Giroux, LLC
ISBN 978–0–89870–932–2
Library of Congress Control Number 2002111117

Printed by Thomson-Shore, Dexter, MI (USA); 583LS225, JULY 2012 ∞

To my mother,
a descendant of Margaret and William Roper

CONTENTS

I

CHANGES FOR A SCHOOLBOY

I T WAS A SUMMER DAY in the year 1490, and, at Saint Antony's School in London, England, afternoon classes had come to an end. A stream of boys ran joyfully into the yard. They were dressed in long, loose shirts fastened with a leather belt; short knickers that were gathered in closely at the leg; and immensely long woolen stockings. Their hair was also very long, reaching almost to their shoulders. They did not carry any schoolbooks because the printing press had only just been invented and books were rare, expensive things.

When the boys had rushed out of the schoolhouse they were followed more slowly by another boy and a man in a black cloak. This man was the schoolmaster, and the boy was twelve-year-old Thomas More. Thomas was not very big for his age. He had thick, light brown hair; a mouth that more often than not was stretched in a grin; and dancing, blue-gray eyes that missed nothing. It was clear that he found it difficult to walk solemnly beside the schoolmaster.

"Well, so this is good-bye, Thomas", said the master, with a smile.

"Yes, sir."

"You've been a good pupil here at Saint Antony's, and I trust you'll go on studying hard under your new tutors. This is a turning point in your life, Thomas. You're leaving school and going to continue your education at the palace of the Archbishop of Canterbury himself. I hope you realize how lucky you are and will make the most of your opportunities. Sir John More, your father, is an excellent lawyer and a highly respected citizen, so you must do him credit."

"Oh, yes, sir, I shall!"

Good-bye now. God bless you."

"Good-bye, sir, and thank you for everything." Thomas grinned at the schoolmaster. Then, after a last glance around the playground, he ran out into the street.

He felt thrilled at the thought that he had just left school and that the future lay before him. He skipped along the narrow, cobbled roadway, kicking happily through the muddy puddles and wondering how to celebrate the occasion.

He came to a street market and paused in front of a cake and candy stall to think what he would buy if he had any money. In a corner of the marketplace two men had organized a cockfight, and for a while Thomas watched the angry birds pecking and clawing at each other. But it was not a pleasant sight, so he soon moved on again. Then, turning a corner, he saw something that really interested him. A huge wagon had been drawn up in the middle of the street, and some men were acting out a play, using the wagon as their stage.

Beginning in the Middle Ages, members of the various trade guilds, or unions (the saddle makers, the blacksmiths, the bakers, and so on) used to celebrate important feast days by performing plays in the streets of London. There were no theaters at that time and, of course, no movies or television, so the street play was the only kind of drama that the people saw—and they loved it.

A big crowd had gathered around the wagon, but Thomas managed to squeeze his way through to the front. The wagon was magnificently decorated with green branches and strips of colored material. Drapes of sacking hung down over the wheels, hiding the space beneath the wagon that formed a dressing room for the actors. They were performing the old, old story of the brave knight who killed a dragon. The knight wore a suit of gleaming armor, and the enormous, wicked-looking dragon had a wooden head painted in brilliant shades of red and green. From time to time real smoke and flames poured out of this marvelous animal's mouth.

Nearly everyone cheered loudly when the play was over, but some were harder to please, and they threw handfuls of mud or rotten fruit at the performers. Thomas, however, was enchanted with the show. When the actors moved on to other streets and other audiences, Thomas followed them for the sheer pleasure of watching the dragon spit flames all over again.

Thomas had seen that street play six times before he realized that it had grown dark and chilly and that he should have been in bed long ago. He realized, also, that Mother Maude, the old woman who had looked after Thomas and his young brother and two sisters since their own mother had died, would be worrying about him. He felt a pang of regret for his selfishness, so, without wasting any more time, he ran quickly toward his home on Milk Street.

"Master Thomas! Where have you been? Your brother and sisters were in bed long ago!" cried Mother Maude sternly as Thomas hurried in. But after she had given him his supper, her eyes lost a little of their stern look.

"And now it's high time you were in bed. Your father's taking you over to Lambeth Palace tomorrow, remember, and if you're half asleep the good Archbishop

Morton will think, 'What sort of a dull boy is this that's been brought to live in my house?' So hurry and say your prayers like a good lad."

Thomas knelt down and prayed silently for a few minutes, while Mother Maude grumbled to herself about the huge holes in his stockings.

". . . And please, God, give Mother Maude a better temper", Thomas ended aloud, with a mischievous glance at the old servant. Then he jumped up and threw his arms around her neck. "Dear Mother Maude, I love you very much, and I shall miss you when I'm living at Archbishop Morton's palace. Will you come to see me?"

"Bless you, Master Thomas, of course I will! But mind you work hard at your lessons and do everything you're told. Come to bed now; since it's your last night, I'll tuck you in."

She lit a thick, greasy-smelling candle from the fire, and they went upstairs together. Within a few minutes Thomas was curled up snugly in bed, listening to the noise of carts and horses' hooves in the narrow, cobbled street outside. He had meant to spend that last night at home lying awake and thinking about all the exciting things a young man could do with his life in the year 1490, but after a few seconds he was sound asleep.

The next day, Thomas said good-bye to his brother and sisters, his stepmother, old Mother Maude, and the other servants at Milk Street. Then he set out with his father for Lambeth Palace, where the Archbishop of Canterbury lived.

It was the custom in the fifteenth century for the children of English gentlemen to be sent to the home of some rich friend of their parents in order to learn the very complicated manners of those days—how to bow or curtsy, for instance, and how to make politely flattering speeches. The children also had lessons in music, mathematics, history, and other subjects, especially Latin. Latin was used for all formal letters and conversations, so it was very important to have a good knowledge of it. These boys and girls were not treated as members of the family in the home where they were sent. On the contrary, they were more like servants, for they acted as pages or handmaids to the master and mistress of the house. This taught them to serve rather than be served, which was very good for them.

Thomas had often heard that Archbishop Morton was an extremely kind and wise man, so he had no fears about going to live at Lambeth Palace. He knew that he would meet other children there, pages like himself, and he felt excited at the prospect of making new friends and experiencing new things.

He hurried along beside his father, and when they came to the broad River Thames, covered with boats of all sizes, he looked eagerly toward Lambeth Palace on the far side. Within a very short time a ferry had rowed them across the river, and they stepped out into the palace gardens.

The gardens were large and peaceful and made a great contrast to the noisy, dirty, narrow streets of London where Thomas had lived all his life. The palace itself looked enormous. Thomas was used to a cramped town house, and all at once he felt rather timid at the prospect of living in such a grand place. He stayed very close to his father as they were shown into the echoing hall. They were left in a small waiting room for a few minutes. Then a man in the long black clothes of a priest—the archbishop's secretary—came to take Thomas to join the other young pages.

"Good-bye, Son", said Sir John More affectionately. "Mind you study hard and do everything you're told."

"Yes, Father. Good-bye", said Thomas, feeling suddenly a little sad. But he had no time to be unhappy about leaving his father, for the secretary whisked him away. They walked along what seemed to be miles of passages—from the grand front part of the palace to the dark and rather smelly servants' quarters at the back. The secretary opened a door; Thomas was pushed through, and he found himself standing in a big, bare room. Two servants looked up, and seven or eight boys turned from their places at a long table to stare at Thomas.

"Hullo! Who are you?" demanded the largest boy.

"Thomas More", he replied, his eyes on the table. The boys were at dinner, and the sight of their food reminded Thomas that he had been too excited to eat breakfast that morning.

"Give him some dinner", called the big boy, and another huge plate of cold beef was brought. "There you are, Mister Thomas More! It's pretty awful, but it's all you'll get here. Well, young fellow, tell us about yourself!"

Thomas was longing to begin his meal, but he put down his knife and turned politely to the boy.

"I was born on February 6, 1478, at Milk Street in the city of London. I've got an older sister and a young brother and sister. I had another brother and sister, but they died. So did my mother, when I was six. I've got a stepmother now."

"And what about your father? What does he do?"

"He's a lawyer. All my people are. He wants me to become one too."

"Become a lawyer? Goodness, what a bore!" The big boy made a face, and all the lads laughed loudly.

"Less noise there, young gentlemen! And hurry up; it's nearly time for His Lordship the archbishop's dinner", called a tall, magnificently dressed man who had just entered.

"That's the head steward", explained the big boy under his breath. "He's only a servant, really, but he works us like a slave driver. You can generally bribe the other servants to do some of your jobs for you, though. And you can get them to buy you some decent food. You'll soon be sick of bread, and beef, and watery beer, I can tell you!"

He turned away abruptly, and at last Thomas was free to begin his dinner. But when he looked down at his plate he was astonished to see it completely empty! Then there was a giggle from his other neighbor, and, glancing at this boy's bulging cheeks, Thomas knew who had stolen his food.

"That'll teach you to talk so much!" chuckled the boy, and Thomas grinned, knowing that the joke was on himself. Then the head steward came to tell him that he was to wait on the archbishop at dinner.

The head steward was such a splendid figure that Thomas expected Archbishop Morton to look even more marvelous. His first glimpse of the old archbishop was a little disappointing, for this famous man was small and thin, with a very wrinkled face. He looked quite unimportant beside his guests, some of whom were dressed as brilliantly as peacocks, with vivid silk cloaks and so many plumes dangling from their hats it was a wonder they could see anything at all. But there was a pleasant twinkle in the archbishop's eye, and Thomas remembered that he had a great reputation for enjoying a joke. Suddenly Thomas felt quite confident that he was going to be happy at Lambeth Palace.

A procession of servants carried huge plates of food to the table, and the dinner began. Thomas was made to feel very hungry again, for there were rich soups, river fish, kidneys cooked in wine, a great boar's head, and the breasts of roasted swans. But it was the guests and their conversation, more than the food, that interested him. He crept closer and closer to hear what they were saying.

The man sitting on the archbishop's right hand was a big red-faced country gentleman. Thomas heard him explain to the archbishop that he had given up growing crops on his land. He was rearing sheep instead and doing extremely good business with the foreign cloth merchants, who bought his wool for a high price.

The farmer seemed very pleased with himself, but the gentleman seated opposite, a solemn-looking person, frowned disapprovingly. He was a lawyer, he said, and every day in the law courts he met men who were suffering because of this general changeover to sheep raising.

The trouble was that when the landowners stopped growing crops, the farm laborers lost their jobs. They came to the city looking for work, but did not find it. When they were desperate with hunger and worry, they fell into temptation and stole. Then, because it was the law, the judges had to sentence these unfortunate men to death for stealing a rich man's purse!

Thomas gave a gasp of horror. Archbishop Morton felt a blast of cold air on his neck. He turned around, and Thomas suddenly found that everybody was looking at him.

"Well, now," said the archbishop kindly, "and who is this blowing down my neck?"

"Trying to make His Lordship catch cold, young fellow?" bellowed the red-faced farmer. "We can't allow that, you know!"

"I didn't mean any harm", said Thomas in a small voice. "I—I was just interested."

"And there's certainly no harm in that," agreed the archbishop, "only, the next time you blow, warn me beforehand, and I'll pull up my fur collar!" He smiled and peered at Thomas. "Ah, yes, you must be the son of my good friend, Sir John More?"

"Yes, sir—I mean, My Lord", said Thomas. "I've come here to learn."

"And I expect a bright lad like you has learned a thing or two already!" nodded the lawyer encouragingly. "What have you learned today, boy?"

Thomas' blue eyes shone mischievously. "Please, sir, I've learned that I must eat my dinner very fast indeed, or someone else will finish it for me."

Archbishop Morton and his guests roared with laughter. Then the head steward pulled at Thomas' sleeve. He remembered that he was only a page and stepped back, leaving the adults to their talk.

Thomas settled down very easily at Lambeth Palace. He was popular with everybody because he was always cheerful and always ready to help someone else. He soon learned to like plain cold beef and bread, and he did not mind the little household jobs that were given him. His lessons he enjoyed thoroughly, as he had done at Saint Antony's, and his tutors gave excellent reports to his father and the archbishop.

Good Archbishop Morton kept a fatherly eye on everyone in the palace, but he took a special interest in Thomas, who from the first had proved himself to be so intelligent. At dinnertime he would often ask Thomas questions on Latin, mathematics, or philosophy to show his guests how well the boy was progressing.

The weeks passed from summer to autumn. Then winter came, and the dark kitchen passages began to smell of all sorts of delicious things as the Christmas pies and cakes were baked. The pages spent their free time helping to make costumes for the play that was acted by members of the staff in every big household at Christmastime. On Christmas Eve huge loads of evergreens were carried in from the palace grounds, and the children were given the pleasant task of decorating the great hall.

Later in the evening everybody went to Midnight Mass in the palace chapel. The beauty of that Mass so filled Thomas with joy and love for the Infant Christ that he would have been quite content if Christmas had consisted of nothing more. However, when the time came, he took his part as eagerly as anyone in the feasting and the fun.

There were three whole holidays for Christmas, and the one that Thomas enjoyed most was the last—the feast of Saint Stephen. On that day it was the tradition for masters and servants to treat each other as equals and for everyone who possessed anything at all to give it to someone else.

Early in the morning Mother Maude arrived with a dozen of her special spicy cakes. Thomas was very glad to see his old nurse again, and they chatted happily until it was time for Mother Maude to leave.

On his way back from seeing her out of the palace gate, Thomas passed the kitchens, where crowds of very poor people were waiting to receive the customary Saint Stephen's day gifts of food. For a long while Thomas watched, knowing that at houses and farms all over England huge pies just like these were being cut up and handed out to the poor of the district.

Some of the beggars in line had the faces of countrymen, and suddenly Thomas remembered his first day at the palace, when the archbishop's lawyer friend had talked about laborers who could not find work. He quickly untied the cloth bundle in his hands and began to give away Mother Maude's spicy cakes. There were only twelve of them, and they were soon gone, but Thomas hoped that he had done something to help a few hungry men and maybe prevent their having to steal.

Throughout his whole life Thomas would remember the poor until he became known everywhere in the country as their best friend.

Dinner on that Saint Stephen's day was eaten in the great hall, with the whole household present, from the archbishop down to the youngest kitchen boy. There was plenty of delicious food, and, to make quite sure the party was a success, a professional comedian had been hired. Thomas loved a joke almost more than anything, so immediately he and the comic became firm friends.

After dinner came the high spot of the day, the Christmas play. It was to be acted by the servants, with the professional comic to help them along. But where was this man all of a sudden? Thomas could see no sign of him. Then he heard his own name called, and there, half-hidden behind a curtain, stood the comic, looking very green in the face.

"Thomas, I feel awful! It must have been something I ate", he groaned. "I can't possibly take part in the play. Whatever shall I do?"

"Don't worry! Quick, lend me your cap, and everything will be all right", said Thomas eagerly.

A few moments later the play began. It was a cheerful Christmasy piece, working as usual around the story of Saint George, the patron saint of England, and the dragon. There were several other very entertaining characters, including, of course, the clown. But a most extraordinary thing had happened. This clown, skipping around the room and raising shouts of laughter with his wisecracks and his antics, seemed suddenly to have shrunk into a very little fellow indeed.

"Why, it's Thomas!" cried someone.

"Yes, it's Thomas!" cried the rest. Then there was more applause, and Thomas had to go up to the high table to be congratulated by the archbishop's guests.

"That's a smart lad", remarked one of them.

"He is indeed", nodded the archbishop, who was still dabbing tears of laughter from his eyes. "Yes, believe me, that child will grow up to be a marvelous man!"

Already, at the age of twelve, Thomas More had shown himself to be remarkably quick and clever, as well as full of fun. From then on the wise archbishop took an even greater interest in his progress. He was an extremely fortunate boy, for, besides being the Archbishop of Canterbury, Archbishop Morton was also the Lord Chancellor of England. That is to say, he was the king's right-hand man and the chief person in the country after the king himself. Therefore, living at Lambeth Palace was, to Thomas, what living at the White House would be to an American child.

Thomas stayed at Lambeth for about two years. Then, when he was fourteen and could speak Latin as easily as English, Archbishop Morton told Sir John More that he was so pleased with the boy he wanted to send him to Oxford University.

This was a completely new idea for Sir John. None of the More family had ever been to a university. Sir John was not sure that he wanted his son to be sent so far away from home and live among young men who might lead him into all sorts of mischief. However, he realized that the archbishop was doing Thomas a great favor and that this was not an opportunity to be missed. He thanked the archbishop and gave his consent.

Thomas was thrilled when he heard that he was to be sent to Oxford. Sir John warned him that he would not have much pocket money to spend because he did not intend any child of his to grow up an extravagant waster. But Thomas was too excited to care about being short of money. He hardly had time even to feel sad at the thought of leaving his friends in Lambeth Palace.

Thomas' life at Lambeth had been fairly strict, but at first he certainly found Oxford life a great deal harder.

He arrived in the beautiful city after a long horseback journey from London and made his way to Canterbury College, where he was to live and study. A porter showed him up to his room. It was tiny and cold, lit by two narrow windows with no glass in them. When Thomas' eyes had grown used to the dimness, he saw four young men working away by the windows. They wore their coats and were bending over their books in order to catch the last of the daylight. Thomas said, "Good evening", and they turned around.

"Sh! You mustn't speak English!" hissed one of the students. "If you're caught speaking anything but Latin you'll be fined a farthing!"

"Goodness, I must remember that", replied Thomas in Latin. "I've got only a penny a day allowance for everything, including my food."

"A *penny*! That's a bit mean, isn't it?" exclaimed another of the students.

"Not really", Thomas grinned. "My father just believes in teaching us to be economical."

"He certainly does! Well, before you waste any of your precious penny, we'd better tell you about the fines. The rate for not going to Mass, or vespers, or matins is a penny, and for fighting with swords or sleeping out of college it'll cost you fourpence. If you're caught, that is!"

"And there are hundreds more fines, so you'll have to be very careful", put in a third student. "But, in any case, a penny won't go far. You'd better do as some of the poor students do and ask the chancellor of the university for a license to beg in the streets."

"Oh, I don't think my father would approve of that!" laughed Thomas. "Still, I expect I shall manage all right on my penny. But even if it costs my whole week's allowance, I *must* have something to eat now. When is supper?"

"It's over, I'm afraid", said the first student. "All the meals are early here, you see, because we get up before five in the morning and start work at six. Then we go to bed soon after nine to save candles and get warm. But never mind. Supper was only watery soup, as usual. I've got some bread you can have, and some homemade wine."

"Thank you very much", said Thomas. "I'd be glad of your bread, if you can spare it. I'd prefer not to start at Oxford on a completely empty stomach!"

For the next two years Thomas was continually hungry. He was often cold as well and always poor. But in spite of the hardships he was very content at the university, where he made many friends among the students.

Thomas was growing up into a brilliant young man, and, as he progressed with his studies, he found a whole new world of learning opening out before him. His remarkable intelligence began to attract the attention of some of the Oxford professors. Soon they, also, were his friends, and Thomas was spending more and more of his leisure with them, absorbed in some learned discussion. Sir John More need not have feared that his son would

waste time, money, or anything else at the university!
However, when he paid a visit to Oxford he was shocked
to hear that Thomas had got himself into debt.

"Only for twopence, Father", said Thomas cheerfully,
cutting short Sir John's angry exclamations. "Look, I've
kept a daily account of everything I've spent, as you told
me to, so you can see for yourself. I'm sorry I didn't have
enough money to send the accounts to you."

Sir John took the sheets of paper and frowned over
the items. Dinner, a halfpenny; supper, a farthing;
candles, a farthing; and so on. Then he glanced up.

"You bought a notebook on Tuesday and another on
Wednesday. Why two?"

"The second one was for Greek."

"*Greek?*"

"Yes, Father. Some of us here are terribly interested in
this 'new learning' that has just been introduced into
England. For one thing, Greek makes it possible for us
to read so much ancient literature that has never been
translated."

"Now listen to me, Thomas", exploded Sir John. "His
Lordship, Archbishop Morton, sent you here to Oxford,
and very good it was of him. But if either you or he
thinks that I am going to let you waste your time studying useless things like Greek, then you're wrong! Greek
is for people like priests and monks who are going to
spend their lives reading books. Now I know most of the
students here are preparing to enter the Church, but
you're *not*. I mean you to come back to London and

become a respected lawyer, as I am, and there's no room for Greek in a busy lawyer's life! So forget all this non-sense and work at the subjects that are going to be of some use to you!" Sir John paused and glared at his son. "Well? Have you got anything to say?"

"Yes, Father", Thomas grinned and raised his feet from the floor so that Sir John could see the holes in his boots. "Please, can I have some money to get my boots mended?"

Sir John gave him the extra money and then returned to London. But Thomas was not left to enjoy his Oxford life very much longer. One day in 1494, when he was sixteen and had been at Canterbury College barely two years, he received a letter from home that made his usually happy face look glum. His father wrote that he considered Thomas had spent long enough at the uni-versity. He was to come back to London at once and start studying to be a lawyer.

When Thomas' friends heard the news, they were very indignant and declared that Sir John More must be a stupid man to wish to spoil his son's brilliant university career. Thomas shook his head. He reminded them sadly that it was natural enough for a father to want his son to become a rich, successful citizen rather than an un-known scholar. He took his disappointment very well, but he could not pretend that he wanted to leave Oxford.

2

A YOUNG LAWYER AND
THE HOUSE OF PARLIAMENT

THOMAS PACKED UP HIS BOOKS and the few shabby
clothes that he possessed and returned to dusty,
smelly London. He was an understanding young man, so
he did not feel bitter at being taken away from the
university. He realized that Sir John had been acting only
for his good and had, in fact, planned his future very
carefully.

In those days a university education was intended chiefly for young men who were going to become monks or priests. For an Englishman who wanted to get on in the world, the best way to success was training at the London law courts, which were famous all over Europe. These courts were divided into several departments called inns, and at each inn about two hundred students trained to become lawyers. Sixteen-year-old Thomas was sent to study at New Inn. *obedience*

He had no interest in law, but he knew how much his father wanted him to do well, so he worked very hard for his father's sake. After about two years at New Inn he was promoted to a bigger court named Lincoln's Inn. He passed all his examinations with great honors, and finally he became qualified. He had now finished his training and was ready to accept as his client anybody who had become involved in a court case and wanted a lawyer to represent him.

Meanwhile, Thomas had not forgotten his university friends. They wrote long letters to each other, and there were happy reunions when any of them visited London. Thomas' Greek teacher soon came to live in the city, and Thomas was delighted to be able to start studying with him again.

Sir John More was a judge at Lincoln's Inn, so Thomas was very closely under his eye. Sir John was not pleased when he realized how much Thomas was seeing of his learned companions from Oxford and how often he had his head in a Greek or theology textbook. He could never be persuaded that the "new learning" was not a waste of time. He grew so annoyed with his son that at last Thomas decided the only solution would be for them to see less of each other. One evening at supper he announced that he planned, with Sir John's permission, to go and live away from home for a while.

"Live away from *home*, Son?" exclaimed Sir John. "Whatever for?"

"I just think it would be better for all of us."

Sir John knew exactly what Thomas meant. He grunted and growled, then asked where Thomas intended to live.

"With the Carthusians in the Charterhouse, Father."

"The Charterhouse!" cried Sir John in horror. "You mean you're going to live among a lot of priests and monks? Why, boy?"

Thomas smiled. He could never resist teasing his father.

"Well, for one thing, it'll be much cheaper than living in ordinary lodgings. I don't expect you'll increase my allowance when I move out of here!"

"I certainly will not!" snorted Sir John. "But is that your only reason for choosing the Carthusians? You're not thinking of taking religious vows yourself or any nonsense of that sort?"

This was the question Thomas had been dreading. But he faced it bravely and looked straight at his father.

"I don't know. That is what I am going to find out. I'm not sure if I have a vocation or not."

"Of course you haven't! You mustn't! I shan't allow it!" cried Sir John in genuine panic. Then he made a great effort to control himself and went on more quietly. "Listen. We Mores are lawyers, good lawyers. We've worked our way up and got to be respected. We're plain, honest citizens, Thomas. We don't make priests, and we don't make brilliant scholars, either. So, if you've any fancy notions about becoming a famous theologian or a bishop, the best thing you can do is to forget them! They won't bring you anything but poverty. My word, I'm sorry I ever let His Lordship send you to Oxford at all if this is what it's done for you! Now be a sensible lad and concentrate on your legal work. I've got great hopes for you, and you don't want to disappoint me, do you?"

"No, Father, you know I don't! But I must do what I feel is right", insisted Thomas. "I'm sorry if it upsets you, but I must find out whether I have a vocation."

"Very well then, go!" snapped Sir John. "But if you must go, at least have the sense to take a good thick cloak with you. Those monasteries are bitterly cold."

Sir John was very worried, and he would have been even more worried if he had realized how hard a life Thomas was going to lead at the Charterhouse. Thomas was out to test his vocation, and he did not intend to make things easy for himself.

As far as his work in the law courts would let him, he lived exactly like one of the monks. He slept in a tiny cell, he fasted, and he got up to say the Office in the middle of the night as well as very early in the morning. He also inflicted many secret penances on himself— sleeping on a bed of planks with a block of wood for his pillow and always wearing a horsehair shirt that was so rough to his skin it often made him bleed. Naturally, under those conditions, he did not get much sleep. But that was according to plan because it meant he had more time for prayer and the studies that interested him so much.

Thomas was extremely happy among the Carthusian monks, but he could not make up his mind whether or not he should spend the rest of his life with them. That, of course, would mean going against all of his father's wishes, which he did not want to do. However, the most important point was this: Did God intend Thomas for the life of a clergyman or a layman? Thomas thought and prayed continually about his vocation, and he talked over the matter with his closest friends.

One of Thomas' oldest and dearest friends was Cardinal Morton himself. He had been created a cardinal while Thomas was at Oxford. Thomas was very grieved when he died, but he never forgot the saintly old man or the many lessons he had learned from him.

Thomas had a great deal of thinking to do before he could decide about his future. One day, as he was walking along the street, he was so absorbed in his thoughts that he bumped right into another young man.

"Ouch! Look out, sir. Why, it's Thomas More!"

"Lord Mountjoy! How nice to see you again!" cried

Thomas, clasping his friend's hand. "How are you after all your travels? I didn't know you were home again."

"Yes, and guess whom I've brought with me— Erasmus!"

"Desiderius Erasmus, the Dutch monk?" asked Thomas excitedly. Erasmus was a great scholar and writer, and his name was well known to the little group of Englishmen who were absorbed, with Thomas, in the "new learning". "Oh, I should very much like to meet him!"

"You shall. He wants to meet you, too", said Lord Mountjoy. "I hope he's going to make a long stay here in England. The poor fellow has had very bad luck. Since the Pope gave him permission to leave his monastery he's had a terrible time trying to earn a living and carry on with his own writing. As you know, I was brought up as a schoolmate for the king's second son, Prince Henry, so I've got quite a lot of influence with him. I mean to try and get him interested in Erasmus. But, listen, you and your father must come and see us. We're staying at my father-in-law's for a few days, then we're going to our country house at Greenwich, so come as soon as you can. I know you and Erasmus will like each other!"

Erasmus, the Dutchman, was about twelve years older and quite different in character from high-spirited Thomas. Life had always been hard and unhappy for him, and, as a result, he had developed into a bitter, disappointed man, extremely sensitive and often irritable. But he was as brilliantly clever and witty as Thomas himself, and they became friends at once.

As they walked together in the gardens of the Mount-joy home, Erasmus confided in Thomas, telling him about his ambitions.

" 'I want to help reform the Church", he said. "For one thing, I mean to study the Holy Scriptures in the Greek in which they were originally written, then tell people about Christ's laws in words they can really understand. You know how bad the present Latin translations are."

"Yes, indeed", agreed Thomas. "It's no wonder some people don't know what to believe or how to act. What a tremendous thing if a good translation of the New Testament could be put into everyone's hand!"

"Exactly! That's just what I want to do. And that's why Greek is so important. There are hundreds of valuable books and documents to be read that haven't been translated yet. With a knowledge of Greek we may discover all sorts of things! But, oh, dear, it's all so difficult", sighed Erasmus, falling into one of his fits of gloom. "You don't know how difficult it is, wandering about Europe trying to earn enough money to live on and with no home or family behind you."

"Oh, it's not so bad as that! You've friends in England now, and we'll do everything we can to help you", declared Thomas, feeling suddenly tremendously excited. The talk with Erasmus had made him even more enthusiastic for his studies of Greek and the "new learning". Already he was thinking how wonderful it would be if he could help even in the smallest degree to reform the Church and put people on the right road toward God.

Thomas and his friends did their best to find work for Erasmus that would keep him in England. But he was difficult to please, and nothing that was offered would suit him. He soon grew restless, then he was off on his travels again. However, he and Thomas remained firm friends for the rest of their lives, and during the long spells of separation they cheered and encouraged each other with their amusing letters. Thomas and Erasmus had the same delightful sense of humor that could poke fun at all manner of things.

There was one point on which they could never agree. Erasmus had been forced into a monastery when he was very young, and he had had some most unhappy experiences. He hated monastic life, while Thomas longed for it.

"I simply can't think what attracts you!" declared Erasmus. "Here we are, at the beginning of the sixteenth century, living in a most exciting time when all sorts of progress are being made. And you, a lively, gifted young man, want to shut yourself away from it all!"

"Well, you know how I hate being a lawyer. And, even more, how I hate city life, where everyone's busy serving the flesh, the world, and the devil!" replied Thomas, but Erasmus paid no attention.

"It isn't even as though the clergy were any inspiration to you. Nowadays they lead wickeder lives than all the ordinary people put together! All through Europe it's just the same. Monasteries and convents have become luxurious palaces, and even the bishops think about nothing but getting rich!"

"Yes, you're quite right", Thomas sighed. "They preach fine sermons, but everyone knows that they practice just the opposite of what they preach. Still, one shouldn't be put off by their bad example. I know that if I did become a priest I'd do my utmost to be a good one, to try to make up for the rest. The trouble is, I don't know that I could live up to the high standard that Christ has set for his priests. And the thought of giving up married life is terrible. I do so long for a wife and children and a home of my own!"

"Hm! Out of the frying pan into the fire!" grunted Erasmus, who disliked the idea of marriage almost as much as he disliked the life of a monk. "Well, Thomas, whatever you decide, take your time about it and don't do anything rash."

Thomas was very sensible, so he did take his time. He had been living with the Carthusians at the Charterhouse four whole years before he came to the conclusion that he was unworthy to take Holy Orders and that his true vocation was to remain in the world. In many ways this was a bitter disappointment to him, but he accepted God's will without question and told himself that it was better to be a good layman than a bad priest. He said an affectionate good-bye to the kind Charterhouse monks and took rooms at Lincoln's Inn, where he was working.

Even after he had left the Charterhouse, Thomas kept

up his habits of prayer and penance. He had gotten into the practice of sleeping only a few hours a night, so when he had finished his day's work at the law courts, he still had plenty of time for his studies.

Thomas' studies of the "new learning" had been absorbing him more and more. In addition to reading Greek, he practiced hard at writing Latin. One of his favorite relaxations was to compose humorous little Latin poems for the amusement of his friends!

These learned men began to realize that they had a genius among them. Already the brilliance of young Thomas More was being talked about by scholars as far away as Italy and Spain. In 1501, when he was only twenty-three, he was asked to give a series of lectures in one of the big London churches, before a congregation of much older and wiser men. That was a frightening task for someone so inexperienced as Thomas, but he made a great impression on all who heard him.

Sir John More, however, was not at all pleased about his son's activities. He did not realize that Thomas could get through far more work than most people, and he considered that for Thomas to think about anything but law was a waste of time, as well as of all the money spent on his training. In order to make him concentrate on his career he stopped Thomas' allowance completely. Sir John was not a mean man. He just believed that he was acting for Thomas' good.

"You'll live to thank me, my son, when you're a rich, respected citizen!" he declared sternly.

A rich, respected citizen! A picture came into Thomas' mind of a fat man weighed down by heavy silk cloaks and gold chains and with his eyes glued to a law book. That was the last thing he wanted to be.

Thomas was so intelligent and so economical he probably could have scraped along somehow without his father's allowance. But that would have meant defying him completely and probably ruining the deep affection between them. Thomas loved his father very dearly, so even though it meant a sacrifice, he put aside his own interests for a while and concentrated on law, as Sir John wished.

For the next three years he continued to make good progress in his dull work at the law courts. Then, in 1504, something exciting happened. Thomas was elected a Member of Parliament.

The English Parliament is divided into two parts. There is the upper house, known as the House of Lords, to which all dukes, earls, bishops, and so on have the right to belong. And there is the House of Commons, to which representatives of the ordinary people are elected.

Twenty-six-year-old Thomas was elected a member of the House of Commons, and then Sir John More felt really proud, even though it did not seem likely that such a junior member as Thomas would play a big part in that particular session of Parliament.

Nowadays Parliament meets regularly, but in Thomas' time it met only when the king summoned it. The king at that time was Henry VII.

In many ways Henry VII was a very wise and clever man, and he had done a great deal for England. He had saved it from civil war, and he had helped English merchants by improving trade conditions with foreign countries. But he was rather greedy about money, and the older he grew, the more money he wanted. When Henry VII ordered Parliament to meet, it was usually to tell the members that they must organize another grant of money for him.

In 1504 Henry VII felt that he was very much in need of money. The year before he had married his daughter, Margaret, to the king of Scotland. In 1501 his eldest son, Prince Arthur, had been married to a beautiful Spanish princess named Catherine of Aragon. Prince Arthur died tragically a few months after his marriage, but his father had had all the expense of the wedding. And, in those days, to arrange a suitable marriage for a royal prince or princess was indeed a very expensive business! Henry VII looked at his empty cash boxes and then ordered a meeting of Parliament.

The English people knew their king, and they knew that he had big ideas about money, so they waited very anxiously to hear how much he wanted them to pay.

"Well, son, what's the news?" Sir John More asked Thomas after the first day of the session.

"The news is that His Grace, King Henry, expects ninety thousand pounds to pay Princess Margaret's wedding expenses!" replied Thomas grimly. Sir John gave a gasp of horror.

"Ninety thousand pounds! But that's fantastic! If the king goes on taxing us like this there won't be a man in England with two pennies to rub together! What do the members of Parliament say?"

"We're debating whether to pass the grant or not", said Thomas. "Of course, everyone thinks it's quite unreasonable, but the trouble is that there's nobody who dares to stand up against the king. The members don't like it, but they're more or less agreed that he'll have to have his money."

"Oh, he'll have to have it, all right", nodded Sir John gloomily. "It would be madness for anyone to go against King Henry's wishes. He wouldn't think twice about chopping off his head! Oh, well, we'd better start economizing, I suppose."

All Englishmen felt as Sir John did. They did not want to pay, but they realized that they probably would have to. The members of Parliament met for their last debate with very long faces. About the only cheerful person in London that day was the king himself.

Henry VII sent one of his councilors to listen to the debate and waited confidently for this man to come back and tell him that the grant had been passed. But time went by, and there was no sign of the councilor. The king began to get impatient. Then at last the door flew open, and the councilor came rushing in, his eyes starting out of his head.

"Your Grace! A *beardless boy* has ruined everything for you!"

"*What!*"

"Please, Your Grace, it was a new member, Mr. Thomas More", panted the councilor. "The debate was going very nicely in Your Grace's favor. Then this young man got up and argued so strongly against granting the amount of money you asked for that in the end he won around the whole House to his way of thinking. They're going to let you have only forty thousand pounds!"

Henry VII swore loudly and fiercely.

"Who is this young man who dares to defy me?" he roared, puffing and blowing with rage. "This Thomas More, who is he?"

Fourteen-year-old Prince Henry, who had been reading by the window, looked up with interest.

"I remember him, Father! Bill Mountjoy brought him and that Dutchman, Erasmus, to see me once. I was quite young then."

"Mr. More is Sir John More's eldest son, Your Grace", said the councilor. The king snarled angrily.

"Ah! Then Sir John had better start saying his prayers for his son. I'll have this Thomas More executed!"

"Oh, don't do that, Father! I rather liked him."

"Well, I'll get my revenge somehow!" cried Henry VII, stamping around the room. "I'll take everything he owns. I'll ruin him!"

"Please, Your Grace, I don't think he's got very much to take", explained the councilor. "He's only just started as a lawyer. He's very young, you see."

"Then I shall make his father pay!" shouted the king,

and he continued marching up and down, planning how he could get back at the More family.

A few days later poor Sir John More was taken suddenly from his comfortable house and locked up in the Tower.

The Tower of London, situated in the heart of the city, on the north bank of the River Thames, was one of the king's palaces. But it was not at all like the other royal palaces, with their splendid, airy rooms and beautiful gardens. The Tower had thick stone walls and narrow slits of windows and was, in fact, more a fortress than an ordinary palace.

At times when there was serious rioting or other trouble in England, the royal family shut itself up in the Tower for safety. The king's bodyguard and his own little army had their headquarters in the Tower, and the royal armor was kept there. Another part of London Tower was used as a prison for the king's enemies, or anybody who had committed some offense against him—from a man who owed him a few pounds to a man suspected of plotting to kill him.

Even nowadays a visitor to the Tower of London must shiver to see the grim place and imagine what the jail must have been like when it was in use.

The thick stone walls kept in the damp, and the tiny windows, only a few inches wide, kept out all light and warmth of the sun. The prisoners' cells were tiny, cold, and evil smelling because of the rats and mice that inhabited them. The prisoners had to sleep on thin straw mattresses and eat food that a farmer would have given to his pigs. Many died as a result of the bad conditions long before their prison sentences were over.

It was to this dreadful place that poor Sir John More had been sent. As soon as Thomas heard the news, he got permission to visit his father and hurried to the Tower.

Sir John was busy writing letters of protest to all his friends who had any influence with the king. At the same time he was trying to make out a list of the clothes and food and other comforts that he wanted brought in to him. He was very angry, and the sight of Thomas did not improve his mood.

"Now see what you've done!" he declared. "If you hadn't behaved like a hotheaded young idiot, this would never have happened!"

"But what has happened, Father?" exclaimed Thomas. "Why have they put you in jail? What's the charge?"

"There isn't one! Not really. His Grace, the king, picked a quarrel with me over absolutely nothing at all! Then, before I knew where I was, he'd clapped me in here with orders that I'm to stay till I've paid him a fine of a hundred pounds. A hundred pounds! I ask you, where's a plain citizen like me going to find so much cash?"

A hundred pounds of English money in the sixteenth century would be worth several thousand American dollars today. Thomas looked grave.

"It *is* a lot of money. But don't worry, Father! We'll manage to get it somehow. I'll go and see our friends."

"No, you'd better let me handle this. You'll only make matters worse with your tactlessness. I'm suffering for that already!" snapped Sir John. "Well, Thomas, I suppose you know you've ruined yourself? His Grace won't forget this business, and he'll see you suffer, too! Bah! To think of all my trouble and expense getting you on your feet in our profession! All of it wasted! Oh, go along home, boy. The very sight of you makes me furious!"

"All right", said Thomas, very distressed to think that he was the cause of this terrible situation. "Father, isn't there *anything* I can do?"

"Yes. Tell one of the servants to bring me my fur-lined cloak, a soft pillow, and as much food as he can carry. This prison swill wouldn't nourish a fly! And some good strong beer; I need it! What *you* need, my lad, is a sensible wife to take you in hand!"

Sir John's fine was soon paid, and he was released from the Tower prison. But, naturally, he did not forget his mortifying experience in a hurry, and he continued to tell Thomas that it would be a very good thing if he got himself safely married.

On this point father and son agreed with each other entirely. Thomas had never had any doubt that he would like to marry. It was partly for that reason that he had given up his ideas of a religious life. Now Thomas decided that it was high time to find himself a wife. That summer of 1504 he spent a great deal of his leisure riding out on horseback to the country house of a certain Mr.

Colt, who had several extremely pretty and pleasant young daughters.

Sir John More felt very relieved, for at last it seemed that his son was going to settle down. As a family man, Thomas would surely be too busy with home affairs to get himself into any more trouble.

3

WIFE AND FAMILY—AND ANOTHER

Thomas chose for his bride the eldest of the Colt sisters, seventeen-year-old Jane. Jane was small and very attractive, and she loved to laugh as much as Thomas did. They were married at the beginning of 1505 in the little country church near her home.

Directly after the wedding celebrations, Thomas wrapped Jane snugly in a thick cloak and rode with her back to London. It was not the custom to go away on a honeymoon in those days because traveling was a difficult, unpleasant business—and often dangerous if there were highway robbers about.

Thomas had a home ready and waiting for his young wife at Bucklersbury, a district in the middle of the city. It was crowded and noisy there, and at first Jane missed the countryside very much. However, she soon discovered that there were exciting things to be seen in a city, and she grew to like Bucklersbury, with its strange, sweet smells from the many herb shops that were located in the area.

Like every newlywed couple, Thomas and Jane had their difficulties, but, with Jane's sweet nature and Thomas' kindness and good humor, they settled down perfectly together.

In 1505 the first daughter, Margaret, was born. A year later came Elizabeth, then Cecily, and by the spring of 1508 a fourth child was expected. Thomas and Jane loved their children, and Sir John More was the proudest grandfather in all England.

The young Mores' many friends enjoyed visiting them because it was pleasant to see such a happy family. As for Thomas, he loved being able to have open house for his scholar acquaintances, who had not been very welcome at his father's home. He taught Jane to understand Latin so that she would not be left out of the conversations.

"We are lucky having so many nice people come to see us, aren't we?" remarked Jane one day. She was nursing baby Cecily while Elizabeth played with a doll and Margaret stood by her father's side watching him write a letter.

"We certainly are lucky", agreed Thomas, as he smiled down at little Margaret.

"She can count up to ten now!" said Jane proudly. "You must write and tell Mr. Erasmus what a great little scholar we have in the family! Is it Mr. Erasmus you're writing to now, Thomas?"

"Yes, dear", he replied. It was obvious that Jane felt in a mood to talk, so he put down his pen. "I'm writing to tell Erasmus about my plans for a trip I've got to make. I'm going over to France, Jane. I'm paying a little visit to the universities at Paris and Louvain."

"Going away to France? Oh, Thomas! Then what they're saying must be true!" wailed Jane, suddenly bursting into tears.

"Jane, dearest! What's the matter?" exclaimed Thomas. "What are they saying?"

"That the king has never forgiven you for making Parliament refuse to grant him money. And, so long as he's angry with you, nobody dares bring legal business to you or be too friendly with you in public", sobbed Jane. "They're saying that it isn't safe for you to stay in England any longer because the king is planning to do something terrible to you. Is it true, Thomas?"

Thomas went over and put his arms around her.

"I'm surprised at you, listening to gossip!" he smiled reassuringly. "It's true the king isn't particularly fond of me, but you know how people exaggerate. I'm thinking of getting work in France because it might be more profitable for us to live over there, that's all. I'm not getting very much business at the law courts, as you know, and it costs a lot to keep a home with three little children in it!"

"And a fourth on the way", added Jane, drying her eyes. "Yes, I know, we do spend a lot of money. I try to be economical—but, oh, dear, I'm afraid I must be a bad housewife!"

"You're a very good housewife!" declared Thomas, determined to cheer her up. "And you're very pretty, too. Why else do you think I married you?"

"Because you thought it would be a shame if I weren't married first, since I'm the eldest in our family! You've often told me you really wanted my sister!" answered Jane, and they both laughed. This tale of his preferring Jane's younger sister was a favorite joke between them.

"Well, now, I must finish my letter to Erasmus", said Thomas at last, when he had made quite sure that his wife was happy again.

"And I must talk to the servant about your clothes if you're going away", said Jane. "I do hope you'll look after yourself properly in France! You must come back safely to us."

Thomas did come back safely. He had found his first visit to the continent of Europe extremely interesting, but he wanted his children to grow up in England, so he decided that he would not move the family abroad unless he had to.

The fourth baby had arrived by this time. To Jane's and Thomas' delight, he was a boy, and they christened him John, after his grandfather. The family settled back into its old routine at Bucklersbury and seemed as ideally happy as any family could be.

But the happiness did not last long. In the summer of 1511, Jane fell ill, and for many weeks Thomas was too busy and worried even to write to Erasmus. The next that Erasmus heard of the Mores was the tragic news that Jane had died. Thomas had lost his dear little wife and was a widower with four babies to look after.

With Jane's death the laughter and gaiety went out of the Bucklersbury house. Thomas knew that there could never be another Jane. Yet, for the sake of his young children, someone had to be found to fill her place in the household. Thomas bore his sorrow courageously and set about finding a solution to his problem.

One Sunday evening, a few weeks after Jane More's death, Thomas' parish priest sat at home reading his Office. There was a knock on the door, and his servant came in.

"Please, Father Bouge, there's a visitor to see you."

"Who is it?" asked the priest, perhaps a little impatiently because it was late and he had had a hard day.

"It's Mr. More, Father."

"Oh! Then show him in", said Father Bouge, who liked and admired Thomas very much. Besides, since his wife had died so recently, Thomas might have come for a chat because he was feeling lonely.

Thomas entered, wearing a dark cloak. As soon as he had received the priest's blessing, he explained the reason for his visit.

"I've come to ask you to do something for me, Father."

"I'll do anything I can, my son."

"Well, this may surprise you", Thomas smiled faintly. "I want to be married at once. To be exact, on Monday."

"*Married* on *Monday*, Mr. More? But . . ."

"I know, it's barely a month since my first wife died. But a month is a very long time for little children, and mine must have a mother. Mistress Alice Middleton is a good soul, and I am sure she'll look after my four very well. She has a small daughter of her own."

"She's been married before, then?"

"Oh, yes", Thomas nodded. "She's not young, Father. In fact, she's rather older than I am. Her husband was a cloth merchant here in the city. He died about two years ago. Her child, Alice, will, of course, be brought up with my little ones."

"Well, I hope you'll be very happy!" declared Father Bouge, still trying to get over his amazement. "It's an excellent plan, I suppose, and I admire you for it. But *Monday*! Why, that's tomorrow. It would be impossible to make the arrangements in time."

"I have a dispensation", said Thomas, drawing out a letter from under his cloak. "My Lord, the bishop, has given me permission to be married at once without any banns having been called."

"Ah, that's different! Then would seven o'clock suit you? There'll be few people about so early, and I expect you want to be married as quietly as possible."

"Yes, we do", agreed Thomas. "Seven o'clock would be excellent. Thank you, Father. Well, I won't keep you any longer; it's late. Good-bye till tomorrow."

"Till tomorrow, Mr. More. And may God bless you both!" said Father Bouge devoutly. Then he showed his rather surprising parishioner out into the street.

Thomas' friends were astonished when they heard about his sudden remarriage. All were very curious to see the lady who had taken Jane More's place so quickly.

Erasmus was still abroad, but he received many reports about Thomas' second wife. These reports were not always very complimentary, but Erasmus could not believe that Thomas would have married a lady so unattractive, stupid, and bad tempered as their friends made out. On his next visit to London, he went straight to Bucklersbury to see this new Mrs. More for himself.

Thomas was expecting Erasmus and came out into the courtyard to welcome him.

"Here I am at last, my dear friend!" cried Erasmus affectionately. "How are you and the family?"

"Oh, we're all very fit. My wife sees to that!" replied Thomas. He was in excellent spirits and certainly looked well. "I'm very lucky, Erasmus. Mistress Alice is a wonderful woman. Of course, I miss my little Jane, but

Mistress Alice is so different there's no comparison. Now you must be tired, so let's go into the house."

They went indoors, and Erasmus was shown up to the guest room that was always given to him, so that he felt it was more his home than anywhere in England. He could not help noticing the marvelous cleanness and neatness of everything.

After Erasmus had unpacked his few clothes and his many books, he went downstairs to the library, where he found seven-year-old Margaret More working away at arithmetic. Erasmus was fond of this clever little girl, and they chatted happily together until a servant came to take Margaret to her dinner. Then Thomas joined his guest. But there was still no sign of Mistress Alice, and Erasmus began to wonder what had happened to her.

"I must apologize for my wife", smiled Thomas, as though he guessed Erasmus' thoughts. "When you arrived she was dressing. Then she went to the kitchen to see about dinner. After that she had to go upstairs to tidy herself again! I tell her that if God doesn't give her hell all to herself, he'll be doing her an injustice, because she certainly earns it with her vanity! Ah, here she comes now."

The curtain over the doorway swished back, and Mistress Alice walked in.

She was small, as Jane had been, but in other ways she was completely different from Jane. She was not at all young or pretty, and her clothes were too elaborate for such a short, plump little woman. But she had gone to as much trouble over her appearance as if she had been a beauty queen. The waist of her dress was so tight that she could scarcely breathe.

Thomas led his wife affectionately into the room. She took a good look at the guest before speaking to him.

"I am sorry I was not here to greet you, Mr. Erasmus, but there have been a hundred things to attend to", she said. Then, turning to Thomas, she continued, "By the way, the mother of that no-good servant you dismissed has been here again. She wanted money, but I gave her some soup and sent her away."

"Quite right, dear", Thomas nodded approvingly. Mistress Alice turned back to Erasmus.

"Well, Mr. Erasmus, do you mean to stay in England now, or are you going abroad again?" she asked. "Really, I can't understand why people choose to live in those nasty, unhealthy foreign countries when England is such a pleasant place!"

"They live there because other countries are not necessarily nasty or unhealthy!" said Erasmus, a little crossly. "Besides, one must go where there is a chance of earning a living. Though *that's* hard to do anywhere, goodness knows!"

"Ah, I can see you're just like my husband. No head for business and no idea how to make the best of yourself!" declared Mistress Alice. "As I'm always telling Mr. More, he's got no ambition."

"Oh, let's not bore our friend with all that!" laughed

Thomas. "In any case, I'm sure it's time for dinner. Erasmus, you must be hungry, and I certainly am!"

They went in to dinner, which was an extremely good meal. Thomas and Erasmus had not seen each other for a very long time, so they talked away about their friends, their jobs, and their progress in their studies of the "new learning". They almost forgot Mistress Alice, but she was busy giving orders to the servants and letting her little eyes dart about the table to make sure that everything was just so. After a while she began to yawn and fidget. Then she interrupted the men's conversation, urging them to eat elaborate dishes that they did not want.

"Really, Mr. Erasmus, no wonder you're so pale if you won't eat!" she exclaimed, when Erasmus, who was very fussy about his food, refused a heavy meat pie. "It's the hardest thing in the world to make Thomas have a square meal, and you seem to be just as bad! Well, at least have some beer."

"Erasmus doesn't like beer. It disagrees with him", said Thomas, highly amused at Mistress Alice's indignation.

"*Disagrees* with him? What rubbish!" she cried. "I can tell you, Mr. Erasmus, our good nourishing English beer has produced more fine men in this one country than will ever exist in the rest of the world! Disagrees with you, indeed!"

Thomas roared with laughter and teased his wife into a better humor. But it was clear that she felt cross with Erasmus, while he was irritated by her. However, it was his duty as a guest to be polite, so he asked her about the children. She smiled and looked much prettier.

"Oh, they're all growing enormous!" she replied. "I'll have them brought down. Then you can see for yourself."

She ordered a servant to fetch the children. Erasmus knew very little about such small people, but he spent a pleasant few minutes with the three More girls and Mistress Alice's daughter because they were so intelligent and well brought up. They seemed to love their stepmother almost as much as their father, and she spoke very tenderly to them.

"I always say John is my favorite", she remarked, picking up a fat, merry little boy of three. "Margaret is going to be the cleverest, but John is the luckiest. He really hasn't any very great brains, you see, so his father won't be able to worry him with all the learned nonsense that he intends pushing into the other poor children's heads. My husband and I are having a great argument", she continued, when the children had been taken away again. "I think that it is quite ridiculous trying to educate girls when all they need to know is how to sew and run a house."

"I disagree with you entirely, madam!" said Erasmus hotly. "I see no reason why girls shouldn't have a good education!"

"Don't try to convince her", smiled Thomas. "You won't succeed."

"You certainly won't!" retorted Mistress Alice. "Greek

and Latin and philosophy for young ladies, indeed! Why, Mr. Erasmus, he even tried to educate *me*! He didn't get far, I can tell you. He wanted me to believe that the earth is round—of all the rubbish! Anyone with a grain of sense knows that we'd fall off into space if it were! No, poor husband, he didn't get very far with educating *me*!"

They looked at each other and laughed, and Erasmus realized how very fond they were of one another.

"My wife makes out to be very disobliging. But actually she's put herself out to learn music for my sake", said Thomas proudly. "She can play the harp now and sing very nicely. We'll have some music after supper, Erasmus. Meanwhile, I promised to take you around to our good friend Lord Mountjoy."

"Where you will jabber more scholarly nonsense, I suppose!" said Mistress Alice. "Believe me, if both of you would take the time you spend on talking and books and use it trying to get on in the world, you'd be richer men! Now I must stop talking and get on with my work. I hope there's everything you want in your room, Mr. Erasmus?"

"Yes, thank you", said Erasmus. Then he added sincerely, "If I may say so, madam, everything in this house seems quite perfect!"

"There, my dear, that's a tremendous compliment, coming from Erasmus!" cried Thomas joyfully, and Mistress Alice flushed with pleasure.

"As my husband often tells me, I'm neither a pearl nor a girl, Mr. Erasmus. But I *am* a good housekeeper!" she declared. "Now if you two are going out, take your cloaks. It looks like rain, and I don't want either of you in bed with colds."

She hurried away, and Erasmus went out with Thomas. Erasmus felt happier in his mind, now that he had met Mistress Alice at last. He knew that she was not pretty or clever and that he and she would often disagree with each other. But he felt certain that she would take good care of Thomas and would be a great help to him during their life together. Erasmus told himself that Thomas was a very lucky man having such a capable wife to rely upon.

4

A NEW KING FOR ENGLAND

ONE DAY IN APRIL 1509, when Jane More was still alive, Thomas' friend Lord Mountjoy called at the house in Bucklersbury. Thomas was in the library, working out household accounts and wishing he had more money to pay for all the things that his big family needed. He looked up as Lord Mountjoy entered and saw at once that he was greatly excited about something.

"Thomas, I've wonderful news!" cried Lord Mount-joy. "Put away your work and get out some wine. We're going to drink to the health of the new king!"

"The *new* king?" exclaimed Thomas. Lord Mountjoy nodded.

"Yes! His Grace, King Henry, died this morning—the old villain. And now my dear Prince Hal is ruler of England!"

Thomas said a sincere prayer for the repose of the soul of Henry VII. Then he threw back his head and laughed, as though suddenly he had not a care in the world.

"Don't think me terribly hardhearted, William. I'm just so relieved! Now that the old king is dead I can stop living in dread of what he might decide to do to revenge himself on me. And I can stop pretending to Jane that everything is going fine for us when it's doing nothing of the sort!"

"It'll go fine all right now, my friend! You'll get plenty of work at the law courts now that people needn't be afraid of angering the old king by doing business with you. No one could be afraid of good-natured Prince Hal!" declared Lord Mountjoy happily. "Oh, Thomas, there's a wonderful future ahead of us all with Prince Hal as Henry VIII of England! I know him pretty well, of course, and I can't think of a single gift or virtue he doesn't have. Believe me, he's an ideal king!"

"He certainly seems very kind and generous", said

Thomas, growing as enthusiastic as Lord Mountjoy. "William, is he really as interested in writers and other scholars as they say he is?"

"Most certainly! Oh, our friends will be looked after, don't you worry!" said Lord Mountjoy, guessing Thomas' thoughts. "I tell you, Prince Hal is an exceptionally well-educated and cultured man. And you can't say that of all the kings this country has ever had! He means to make England famous for her schools and universities. I expect he'll provide the money to build new colleges at Oxford and Cambridge."

"It sounds as though out-of-work professors all over Europe would soon be traveling to England to look for jobs!" laughed Thomas. Then a tremendous idea came into his head, and his eyes shone. "Listen! Why don't we get Erasmus over to England? He's desperately short of money and in need of a job."

"What a splendid notion!" agreed Lord Mountjoy. "Prince Hal is already very impressed with him. He might easily give him a good post. I'll write tonight and invite Erasmus to stay with us, as he did in 1499."

"Tell him England is now the Paradise Island!" cried Thomas happily. He was even more thrilled by the thought of being able to do something for Erasmus than by the knowledge that his own life was going to he easier now that Henry VII was dead.

There was a magnificent funeral for the old king. A few weeks later, young Henry VIII was married quietly to Princess Catherine of Aragon, widow of his brother

Arthur. A fortnight after that, Henry and Catherine were crowned king and queen of England.

Thomas felt so overjoyed he decided he must do something to mark the great event. In those days, a fashionable way of showing pleasure was to write a poem full of compliments to the person concerned. So Thomas sat down and composed a very flattering poem to the new king. When the poem was finished, Thomas went to present it to Henry VIII in person.

At the palace he was shown onto a terrace overlooking the lawn, where a group of court officials were practicing archery. Among them was a young man dressed in green from top to toe. Thomas realized that this was Henry VIII, and, as he watched, he felt extremely proud that such a handsome, athletic youth was his own king.

The practice came to an end, and Henry VIII strode across the lawn toward Thomas. He was chatting with an older man who followed him.

"A very good day to you, Mr. More!" he greeted. "Did you see our practice? I beat the others hollow! They can't aim straight, some of those fellows!"

"Ah, but Your Grace is such a remarkably good shot!" said the other gentleman. He was a tall and very dignified person. He had a proud expression and looked as though he would expect his commands to be obeyed at once, with no questions asked. A large crucifix on his chest showed that he had taken Holy Orders, but his clothes were extremely fine and far more elaborate than the king's simple green outfit.

"This is Mr. Thomas Wolsey, the Dean of Lincoln",
introduced King Henry. "He's a favorite of mine because, when all my other officials are trying to make me
work, my good friend Wolsey says I must enjoy myself
while I'm young, and he takes me off hunting with
him!"

Wolsey gave a thin little smile. It was plain that he did
not like to share the king's company with anyone. He
stared hard at Thomas, as if to ask why he had come to
call. Did he not know that the king had no time to waste
on unimportant London lawyers?

"Oh, oh! The Dean is set to throw you out already,
Mr. More!" laughed Henry.

"In that case I'd better state my business and go!"
replied Thomas, and he smiled because he enjoyed meeting someone as high-spirited as himself. Then he explained that he had taken the liberty of writing a
coronation poem for the new king and had come to
deliver it.

"A poem by Mr. Thomas More! Now that is something worth having!" declared Henry, genuinely pleased.
"Believe me, I have to read through so much dull rubbish it's a treat to see something by a scholar like yourself.
Let me have it, Mr. More!"

Thomas held out the sheet of paper. Henry VIII began to read, and he flushed with delight at the many
compliments that were contained in the long Latin
verses.

"My goodness, Wolsey, Mr. More certainly knows

how to flatter me! According to him, I'm quite perfect. I'm going to end all England's troubles and make her the most wonderful country in the world. So I shall, too!" cried the young king enthusiastically. "I mean to conquer England's enemies once and for all!"

"Ah! That will be the day!" said Dean Wolsey eagerly.

"I shall make English scholars famous all over the world!"

"And England herself the most powerful country in Europe!" Dean Wolsey's eyes were gleaming like the king's.

Thomas looked from one to the other and then said quietly, "Excuse me, Your Grace. But there's one thing to be done that's more important than any of those you've mentioned."

"Indeed, Mr. More? What's that?"

"Establish justice for the poor, Your Grace."

"Mr. More's quite right!" declared Wolsey hastily, wishing that he, instead of Thomas, had made this wise and pious remark. "Above all, Your Grace, we want justice for the poor. Life is very hard for them, and if ever there is any trouble, they always get the worst of it. We must look after the unfortunate people in this country first of all, Your Grace."

"Yes, indeed!" said Thomas. "I'm sure, Your Grace, that God's reward to you would be very great if you did your best to help the poor folk of England."

"I shall do so, Mr. More!" promised Henry excitedly. "And after that I shall make England lead the world! I'll become king of France as well as of England. And one day Wolsey may be pope, which I know very well he'd like! Well, and why not?"

"Why not? If God wills it", put in Thomas gently.

"If God wills, of course, Mr. More. And if God wills, I'm going to do marvelous things for England!"

The eighteen-year-old king laughed aloud and did a little dance of joy. Then he remembered his position and became sober and dignified again. He held out his hands politely to Dean Wolsey and Thomas.

"I must ask both of you to excuse me now. If I don't get down to work, I shall be in trouble with my secretary for neglecting my duty! Wolsey, it's fixed we go stag hunting tomorrow. Good-bye, Mr. More. Thank you again for your poem, and don't think that I shall forget you, because I shall not!"

Wolsey and Thomas left the palace together, telling each other how lucky they were to have such a brilliant and right-minded young king.

As they parted at the palace gate, Wolsey laid his hand on Thomas' shoulder. He meant to speak kindly, but he was a little patronizing.

"His Grace meant what he said. He won't forget you, Mr. More. He has use for men with such an excellent reputation as yours. He asks my advice a good deal, so I shall be able to jog his memory about you from time to time. I don't think you need worry about being short of work in the future!"

"Well, with my big family to feed that would certainly

be a nice worry not to have!" agreed Thomas. He could not help smiling to himself because Wolsey was so very full of his own importance.

From then on business improved steadily for Thomas. People were no longer afraid to have him as their lawyer, and he soon had more work than most men could have got through.

In 1510 there was great promotion for him. He was appointed undersheriff of the city of London. That meant he was the chief legal adviser to the mayor and the sheriffs, so he had a very responsible job. Part of his work was to settle disputes between individual Londoners and the city authorities. He became famous for the extremely efficient, just, and generous way he carried out this duty.

Thomas refused to follow the example of many judges before him and force those who came into court to pay him enormous sums of money before he would hear their cases. He asked his clients for only a very small fee, and then he would take nothing more from them, no matter how long or difficult their business turned out to be. Very often, if they were not well off, he did not charge them anything at all.

Thomas' generosity meant that he did not make much money from any one case. However, he worked so quickly and got through so many cases that he was soon earning a good income.

Thomas had simple tastes, and he spent very little on himself. But he thoroughly enjoyed being wealthy because his wealth meant that he could do much to help others. He could also entertain his friends, which he loved to do, and a warm welcome was always waiting for any of them who wished to stay with him. Though there were no marvelous banquets at the More home, there were many simple little dinners for intelligent guests who considered talk and companionship more important than a tremendous amount of rich food.

For five years Thomas worked away in the city, and he grew extremely popular among the Londoners. Then, one day in May 1515, he went home with some exciting news.

"I can see by your face that something's happened", declared Mistress Alice at once. "Well, come along; tell us what it is!"

"Something certainly has happened. And it will please you, my dear, unless I'm very much mistaken!" smiled Thomas. "His Grace, the king, has appointed some other gentlemen and myself to go on a mission to Flanders."

"A mission for the king! My husband, one of the king's ambassadors!" cried Mistress Alice in delight. "His Grace must think a lot of you, Thomas. It just shows that if only you'd push yourself forward more you could make a fortune for all of us! Was it the king himself who gave you this splendid news?"

"No, dear. His Grace is much too busy. Bishop Wolsey gave me my instructions."

"Your Bishop Wolsey is becoming a powerful man, isn't he?" remarked Erasmus, who was staying at Bucklersbury again. "My friends in Rome say he'll be a cardinal before the end of the year. And I believe he's more or less taken over as lord chancellor here in England."

"He's extremely rich", said Mistress Alice, a little enviously. "Thomas, is his palace as splendid as they say?"

"It certainly is very splendid!" laughed Thomas. "In fact, I felt more impressed than if I were going to see the king himself!"

"And what were the instructions he gave you?" demanded Mistress Alice. "Not that they will mean anything to me. I can't understand a word of politics. All I know is that there are too many wars in Europe!"

"You are right about that, my dear", sighed Thomas, and he became sad for a moment as he thought how far from Christ men had grown with their constant disputes. Then he answered his wife's question. "Bishop Wolsey told me that the ambassadors and I are to go across to Bruges, in Flanders. We're to try to settle some of the trading difficulties between England and Flanders. Wars may begin and end, you see, but unless we're all to grow very poor and be short of a lot of things we need, trade must go on. Now, some years ago, His Grace, King Henry VII, made a very good agreement with the foreign traders. Under certain conditions they were to carry on their business and have their warehouses here in England, and our English merchants abroad were to be allowed to do the same. Unfortunately, things haven't turned out as it was hoped they would, and all sides are arguing."

"Everyone is always arguing!" declared Mistress Alice,

though she herself was as good as anybody when it came to an argument. "Well, you go and settle their quarrels, husband. You're a wise man, and I expect the foreigners will like you. And bring me back a nice piece of Flemish cloth for a dress."

"Be careful, Mistress Alice, or you'll have him in jail for smuggling!" laughed Erasmus.

Then little Margaret More came in, and the news had to be told all over again.

"Oh, how exciting! This is a great honor for you, isn't it, Father?" she cried, and she hugged him hard. Then she sighed. "We shall miss you dreadfully while you're gone! I do hope you'll be all right away from us all."

"I shall be, Meg dearest", replied Thomas, cuddling her gently. "I'm in God's hands, as we all are. You must ask him to bring me back safely and quickly. Meanwhile, I'll expect you to write me long letters to tell me how you're getting on with your lessons. I promise I'll write too. And I daresay I'll be home again before you know it!"

Within a few days Thomas had said good-bye to his family and set off with the other ambassadors.

In Flanders they found themselves very unpopular. It was not difficult to see why. Bishop Wolsey, soon to be Cardinal Wolsey, had some fine qualities, but he was a selfish man. He had taken advantage of the constant wars in Europe and had helped himself to a good deal of Flemish property. Naturally, the Flemish people resented this. Their officials were rude and uncooperative during the long trade discussions with the English.

"This Bishop Wolsey of yours. What right has he to come here and make himself Bishop of Tournai?" demanded one of the Flemings.

"You English!" growled another. "Why can't you stay in your own country?"

"We'd be glad to!" smiled Thomas. "We'll be off just as soon as we've done our business. So, gentlemen, shall we get down to work?"

The unfriendly Flemings were soon won over by Thomas' good humor, patience, and tact. Little by little, some progress was made at the talks, which were held first in Bruges, then in Antwerp. But it was a very slow process.

Thomas had enjoyed exploring the bright, clean-looking Flemish towns. But interesting new sights and acquaintances could not make up for his home life. He missed his family terribly. However, he determined to make the best of things, and he very sensibly decided to fill his leisure with some absorbing work that would distract him from his homesickness.

One day another of the English ambassadors remarked that Thomas seemed to be working very late at night.

"Three times this week I've noticed the light burning in your room well after two!" he remarked. "Whatever keeps you so busy, Mr. More?"

"My accounts!" replied Thomas jokingly. "I'm trying to work out the problem of how to pay my bills without any money. You know, it makes me rather anxious to think of all the good legal work I'm losing while I'm away from London. My family are devoted to me, bless

them, but I can't persuade them to stop eating just because I'm earning nothing!"

"I do understand, Mr. More. His Grace, the king,
must be reminded again about sending your ambassador's
fees", said Thomas' colleague. He knew perfectly well
that it was not accounts that were keeping Thomas at
work far into the night. But he did not like to seem
inquisitive, so he said no more.

Late that evening, the ambassador made an excuse to
call on Thomas at his lodgings. As usual, the light was
shining under Thomas' door. But there was no reply to
the ambassador's knock. He pushed the door open. Thomas was pacing up and down the room, dictating to his
secretary, a young man named John Clement.

"—so, under these conditions," Thomas was saying,
"a man shall be allowed to divorce his wife."

The ambassador gasped with horror.

"Mr. More, what are you thinking of?" he cried.
"Under *no* conditions may there be divorce!"

John Clement dropped his pen, and Thomas swung
around. They both looked like schoolboys caught raid-
ing the store cupboard. Then Thomas grinned.

"Why, sir, this is a surprise! John, go fetch our guest
a glass of wine. He looks as though he needs it."

"Thank you, Mr. More. I do!" The ambassador sat
down and mopped his brow. Thomas laughed heartily

"My poor friend! When you overheard me just then,
did you really believe that the strain of these past weeks
had quite turned my brain so that I had gone against all

the teaching of the Church and was thinking favorably of divorce?"

"Well, Mr. More, I must admit, for the moment . . ."

"Then I'd better explain. I'm writing a story book, and John has insisted on cutting down on his sleep so that he can help me. I got the idea in London. I called it *Nowhere* at first, but now I think I'll fix on *Utopia*. It's about an explorer who discovers a country where life is quite ideal. The inhabitants of Utopia are pagans, so of course they know nothing about God or God's laws. That's why, in very special circumstances, they permit divorce. But for people who don't have the help of the faith, they've organized a way of life about as perfect as it can be."

"It's marvelous, sir!" exclaimed John Clement, coming in with the wine. "There's no poverty in Utopia and therefore no crime. Everyone is equal and works for the general good instead of for himself. The Utopians make a great point of all taking turns at everything—living in town, living in the country, and so on. They take turns at the dull jobs and the interesting jobs, too—except, of course, the specialists. Take me, for instance. I mean to become a doctor one day, and in Utopia I'd be given special facilities to study."

John Clement seemed almost more enthusiastic about the book than Thomas himself. The ambassador sipped thoughtfully at his wine.

"What about the people who aren't strong enough to work?" he asked.

"Oh, they get looked after!" the young secretary

assured him. "There's special food for them in the public dining halls where everyone eats. And those who are really too old or too sick to lead a normal life are sent to one of the hospitals. There are four big, modern hospitals on the outskirts of each town. The whole of Utopia is modern and beautifully planned. But it would take much too long to tell you about it all now, sir."

"Obviously, I must read this book for myself!" smiled the ambassador. "Well, Mr. More, your Utopians certainly seem to have worked out an ideal system for themselves. Do you suppose it would work in Europe?"

"No. Not until men have overcome their selfishness and grown quite perfect. And I don't expect that for a very long time!" answered Thomas sadly. He was silent for a moment; then he said, "To tell you the truth, I *am* hoping that this book will help the people of Europe change their ways a little. They could never carry out the strict system of my Utopia, but it may start them thinking. I pray God it may make them realize how wonderful it would be if everyone lived at peace and worked for each other instead of for themselves."

"I pray God, too!" declared the ambassador sincerely. "This is a wonderful work, Mr. More, and I certainly wish you success! But I'm keeping you from your writing, so I must be off. I shall look forward to seeing *Utopia* in print."

"If ever it is!" laughed Thomas. A few seconds after the ambassador had left, he and John Clement were hard at work again.

Thomas' normal duties kept him so busy that more than a year passed before he finished his book. Then finally *Utopia* was published and was a great success. It brought Thomas fame that lasted all through the centuries—right up to the present day, when people still read it with enjoyment.

In one way, however, *Utopia* did not succeed. Its readers were so absorbed in this fascinating tale of the ideal people that they did not see it as a plan for peaceful, Christian living that they themselves might follow. Thomas had tried hard to bring men a little closer to God. But his attempt had failed, and the terrible wars and wickedness in Europe continued.

5

IN THE KING'S COURT

IT WAS NOVEMBER before the Flanders mission ended
and Thomas could go home. He received much praise
for the way he had handled his share in the trade talks.
Henry VIII thanked him personally and asked Thomas to
come and work for him. Thomas' more worldly friends
were astonished when they heard that Thomas had refused this honor. Dame Alice was highly indignant.

"But, my dear, if I were in the king's pay, I should lose

my independence", Thomas explained patiently. "I should have to do whatever the king wanted me to do, and if, perhaps, it were something I didn't quite agree with, I'd be in an awkward position. Besides, the people of London wouldn't want their undersheriff to be a servant of the king and therefore bound to look after the king's interests rather than theirs."

"Oh, rubbish!" retorted Dame Alice. "The trouble with you is that you haven't a scrap of ambition!"

"Maybe not", smiled Thomas. "Anyway, I like my job as undersheriff, and I don't intend to change it!"

Thomas loved the ordinary folk of his city, as they loved and trusted him. But, during the spring of 1517, they caused him a good deal of trouble.

Many foreign merchants were living in London at this time. The English workers, especially the young trainees, resented them bitterly, for they considered that these strangers were taking business away from them. The small grievance grew into a very big one. It became quite dangerous for a foreigner to go about alone, for fear of being attacked.

On the last day of April, authorities of the city of London heard a rumor that early the following day, May Day, London workers were going to unite and murder all the foreigners. It seemed unbelievable, but, as a precaution, the authorities ordered everyone to stay off the streets after nine o'clock.

Thomas was working late at his office that evening. Suddenly a police sergeant came rushing in.

"Mr. More! Mr. More! The curfew's been broken. There are hundreds of workers all over the city! They're ransacking the foreigners' homes and behaving like madmen! You'd better lock yourself in."

"Lock myself in? I'm going out to talk with them!" answered Thomas, seizing his cloak. The sergeant objected, but Thomas had already hurried out into the street.

There were yelling men everywhere. Thomas was pushed rudely this way and that. He lost his hat, and his cloak was dragged off. But all he cared about was stopping the riot before some overexcited lad set fire to one of the cramped-up wooden buildings and the whole city went up in a blaze.

Thomas turned a corner, and suddenly he saw the main crowd, several hundred strong, rushing like a tidal wave toward him. The leaders recognized him and hesitated. Thomas might have been small, but he looked very dignified and commanding. He stood bravely in the middle of the street as the angry workers surrounded him. Humorously and calmly he tried to reason with them.

"Go back to your homes, good fellows. This is no way for decent citizens to behave."

"England for the English! Turn the foreigners out!" chanted the mob, and the workers jeered loudly when Thomas protested at the idea of turning out England's visitors.

"All right, all right!" cried Thomas above the din.

"Suppose the poor souls were sent packing with their wives and babies. What would you have achieved? You would have proved that rioting and disorder can get you what you want. And under that sort of system you'd find that soon other rioters would come along and put an end to *you!*"

There was so much sound good sense in what Thomas said that the workers were almost convinced. Then, from one of the houses overlooking the narrow street, a pailful of water was emptied over the crowd, and the riot began all over again. Bricks, stones, and handfuls of mud were hurled through the air. A policeman panicked and fired into the crowd. Then the real fighting started.

"Mr. More, sir, you'd best get out of harm's way", urged another policeman. "Cardinal Wolsey has already barricaded himself in his palace."

"Has he, indeed? Well, I'm not going to!" replied Thomas, and as long as the riot lasted he went on trying to restore order.

From the Tower of London heavy guns boomed out over the city. No great damage was done, but the men were frightened. They began to remember Thomas' wise words. Little by little the groups split up. It was three o'clock on a chilly May Day morning, and suddenly everyone wanted to go home. Troops of soldiers and police swept through the city. Soon several hundred workers had been arrested.

That was not the end of the incident. Henry VIII was

furious when he heard about the riot of "Evil May Day", as it came to be called. He declared that the foreign merchants were his guests in England. By insulting them the workers had committed treason and must be punished.

The whole of London was horrified to see gallows erected in the streets and to hear that all the prisoners, many of them still in their teens, were to be hanged publicly. Gentle Queen Catherine, Thomas, and other city officials tried hard to persuade the king to have mercy on the rioters, but he refused.

"We could collect all the prisoners together and then bring His Grace to see them. I'm sure the sight of those poor, silly lads would soften his heart", said Thomas, and the rest agreed eagerly.

A few days later, a tremendously impressive scene was staged in Westminster Hall. All the city officers were present in their formal robes, but it was Thomas himself who spoke to the king on behalf of the rebels.

"These young men are not traitors, Your Grace. They're loyal Englishmen!" he insisted. "If you kill them, you'll be killing some of the finest future citizens! Pardon them, and you won't regret it. Every mother in England will thank you. And God will reward you a hundred times over for your mercy!"

Henry VIII scowled at the four hundred prisoners filling the hall, all weeping and clanking their chains. Then Queen Catherine, dressed in deep mourning and weeping also, came forward to plead with her husband.

At last he gave way and announced a general pardon for the rioters.

A huge cheer went up and continued until the men were hoarse. For the next few minutes Henry VIII thoroughly enjoyed himself as he graciously received their thanks. The true hero, of course, was Thomas, but he had disappeared modestly into the background.

Thomas had behaved most admirably during that whole incident. He had worked hard to quiet the rebels, but when they had ignored him and got themselves into trouble, he worked just as hard to obtain mercy for them. Henry VIII realized this, and his opinion of Thomas More became even higher. He continued to urge Thomas to give up his work in the city and become a court official. But Thomas always refused, very politely and very definitely. Then the hot summer came, bringing an epidemic of the plague, and the king was so busy moving from palace to palace, trying to escape infection, that he had no time to think about anyone but himself.

The plague was a terrible disease, dreaded by everybody because there was no definite cure. It struck very suddenly, so that a man who had been quite well in the morning might be lying helpless by the afternoon, and a few hours later might be dead.

Londoners died like flies in that epidemic of 1517. At night the streets were noisy with the sound of carts taking the bodies away for burial. The Mores lost many dear friends, but they themselves were very lucky.

Though some of the servants fell ill, not one of the family caught the sweating sickness, as it was called.

"I think we're out of danger now, thank God", remarked Mistress Alice one evening. "I hear the plague has moved across the channel to Flanders now. Well, the Flemings are welcome to it, I'm sure!"

Thomas said nothing, and Mistress Alice glanced sharply at him.

"Husband, what are you looking so worried about? The plague has gone to Flanders, I tell you!"

"I know, my dear, and I'm afraid I've got to follow it", replied Thomas. "I'm being sent to Calais as legal adviser on another trade mission."

"To Calais! Oh, no! Just when I thought we were out of danger, you have to go walking right into the middle of it!" wailed Mistress Alice. Because she was so distressed, she began to scold poor Thomas furiously. "I'll be left a widow again, with all these children to look after! And it will be *your* fault! If only you'd go and work for the king, as he wants, you could stay safely with him at his country palaces. Instead of that, you go on being an ordinary lawyer and get sent among a lot of dirty foreigners on these stupid missions! Do you intend to be a stick in the mud for the rest of your life? My goodness, if I had your opportunities, you certainly wouldn't find me hanging back!"

"I'm quite sure I shouldn't, dear!" said Thomas, smiling so kindly and humorously that all at once Mistress Alice's rage disappeared. She apologized and promised to pray to our Blessed Lady to keep Thomas safe while he was abroad.

That mission to Calais was very like the one Thomas had taken part in two years earlier. There were exhausting, boring talks with the Flemings. There were formal banquets that the ambassadors had to attend. And there were constant money worries, because again Henry VIII forgot to send his ambassadors their fees.

In one way, however, that trip was very useful and important to Thomas. It gave him a chance to talk with many wise men and to judge for himself the state of affairs in Europe.

At that time Europe was free from wars for once because the Pope had ordered a five-year truce for all countries. While Thomas was in Calais, he realized that this truce meant a golden opportunity for right-thinking men to put Europe back onto its feet and guide it away from the danger of perpetual wars and wickedness.

Thomas realized, also, that it was up to him, an honest, well-educated man, to help in this work. But he could not play any part in Europe's politics while he was shut away in the London law courts. So he must forget his wish to live a simple, quiet life and must enter King Henry's service.

As he strolled up and down the seashore at Calais, Thomas made his great decision. It meant saying good-bye to what he most enjoyed in life and accepting what he most disliked, but he knew that it was what God meant him to do.

Henry VIII was delighted that Thomas More had at last given in to his wishes. He sent for his new courtier and was very agreeable.

"You won't regret this, I assure you! I look after my friends!" he declared. "I like to have really intelligent men around me, so I'm more pleased than I can say that you're coming to court. Queen Catherine is pleased, too. You're a great favorite of hers! Now, Mr. More, I shall expect you to act as my secretary when I want to write to Lord Chancellor Wolsey and so forth. And I'm going to put you onto my council of advisers."

"I'm very honored, Your Grace. I'll do my best to serve you well", said Thomas with a bow. Henry put a friendly hand on his shoulder.

"Serve me, Mr. More. But serve God first. That's all I ask!"

Serve God first. That was exactly what Thomas intended to do. He left the palace feeling much happier in himself because it seemed that Henry VIII was going to be a good master.

A few days later Thomas had to attend his first meeting of the king's council. Powerful Cardinal Wolsey was at the head of this council and ruled it completely. The councilors did little more than agree to whatever Wolsey said.

On this particular afternoon the meeting started off as usual. Wolsey outlined his plans, and, without asking questions, all the councilors gave their consent. All except Thomas. Strong-minded Thomas did not hesitate to say that he was very much against one of the plans. Cardinal Wolsey was astonished.

"What, Mr. More, you oppose me?" he roared. "You're the only one out of all these wise gentlemen to do so. You must be a fool!"

"Sir, if His Grace, the king, has only *one* fool in his council, he's very fortunate!" replied Thomas promptly.

The cardinal was furious, and he reported Thomas to the king. But he got no sympathy from Henry VIII, who laughed heartily.

Later, Henry sent for Thomas.

"You've upset my lord chancellor properly, Mr. More!" he said with a broad smile. "Well, you may have had an amusing afternoon, but mine's been very dull. You can make it up to me by keeping myself and the queen company at supper. I know you didn't want to come to court, but now that you're here, I'm going to make use of you and enjoy having you around! After supper we might play some music or go up on the roof and take a look at the stars."

"As you wish, Your Grace", said Thomas obediently.

"I'm very interested in the stars, Mr. More", the king continued. "Tomorrow is a feast day and a general holiday, so we might spend it together and go through some new astronomy books that I want you to see."

"Of course, Your Grace. I'd be glad to", replied Thomas. He was going to have to give up his own plans and his precious free time, but that was one of the sacrifices a man had to make when he became a king's courtier.

Henry VIII grew extremely fond of clever, humorous Thomas. He came to rely on his company more and more, until Thomas was spending every spare moment at the palace. The only way he could get an occasional evening with his own family was by pretending to be in a very glum, unsociable mood. Then, for once, the king might let him go home.

Thomas' duties at court meant that he always had to be around in case the king wanted him. When the king traveled away from London to one of his country palaces, Thomas had to say good-bye to his family and go, too.

In June 1520, Thomas had to accompany Henry VIII to France for a very grand meeting with the young French king, Francis I.

The French had asked for this meeting because they were most anxious to be friendly with England and, if possible, to arrange a permanent alliance against Spain. For some time England had been sitting comfortably on the fence between France and Spain, who, as usual, were fighting each other for possession of small states that now are part of Germany and Italy.

However, it was difficult for England to keep out of the European quarrels. For several reasons Henry VIII and his crafty cardinal had almost decided to side with Spain. Spain controlled the Netherlands, where England had important trading business. Also, the

Spanish emperor had influence in Rome, and he could do much toward helping Cardinal Wolsey achieve his great ambition to become pope one day.

Meanwhile, Henry VIII and Wolsey saw no reason why they should not meet the French king. Henry was curious to see his rival, and, in any case, he always enjoyed having a good time. So they would condescend to go across the channel and be expensively entertained by the French. They did not have to commit themselves to anything.

Thomas had to forget that he disliked dressing up so much, because the very best clothes were the order of the day when the royal party set out for France. In a l arge field outside Calais the two kings met. Both were accompanied by hundreds of soldiers, noblemen, and courtiers, each one so magnificently dressed that the meeting place became known as "The Field of the Cloth of Gold". Even the horses wore gold or silver harnesses.

For days on end there were banquets, tournaments, exhibitions of riding, wrestling, and all kinds of sport. Thomas hated to see so much wasteful display, and he was sad because he knew that in their hearts Henry VIII and Francis I were still rivals.

"I don't think much of this skinny King Francis", remarked Henry VIII to Thomas and Wolsey one evening. King Henry was very proud of his own muscular figure.

"Oh, we've got the French eating out of our hands!" chuckled the cardinal. "How disappointed they would be if they knew that we were going straight from this meeting to arrange an alliance with the Spanish emperor, against France!"

Thomas looked gravely at these two men who held England's future in their hands. Then he turned to Henry VIII.

"Please, Your Grace, would it not be possible for our three countries to be friends?" he asked. "The whole of Europe is at war. But in the name of Christianity I beg you to let England do what she can to create peace!"

"What, and lose my name as a great fighter?" demanded Henry VIII. "Lose marvelous chances of wealth and power, as well as my allies, who expect me to join in their wars?"

"It's plain Mr. More hasn't heard the story of the few wise men and the many fools!" said Cardinal Wolsey sarcastically. "The point of the story being, Mr. More, that one can be *too* clever! We should have the whole of Europe turning on us in the end if we kept out of Europe's wars."

"Besides, think of my reputation!" added Henry VIII, puffing out his chest.

Thomas knew that it would be useless to say any more. He was deeply distressed.

A few days later he was ordered off to Bruges for still more trade discussions with the Flemings. He felt very thankful to leave the sickening splendor and insincerity at the Field of the Cloth of Gold.

His business in Flanders was not at all interesting,

but Thomas welcomed the opportunity to be there. Erasmus was staying at Bruges, and Thomas had not seen his friend for a long time.

"I wish you could have decided to settle in England", said Thomas affectionately when they met. "We all miss you so much."

"Oh, well, you know, English life doesn't really suit me", said Erasmus, who was not at all an adaptable person. "Besides, so many of our friends have died of the plague, what would be the point of my living in England? And *you're* as good as dead, Thomas, now that you've buried yourself in King Henry's court! It does grieve me to think of you as a courtier pure and simple, with hardly a minute for the books and studies we used to share. It seems such a waste of a brilliant brain like yours!"

"Well, you see, I'm very fond of the king, which makes me even more unhappy when I watch him growing into a vain and greedy man." Thomas gave a deep sigh. "I'm afraid my lord Wolsey isn't a very good influence on him. I realize now that they're both determined to involve England in as many disastrous wars as they please, just for the sake of more power and glory for themselves!"

"And to think what a short time it is since everyone was saying what a marvelous future England had in store for her with such a perfect young king!" declared Erasmus. "Oh, Thomas, why don't you give up all this business of court life and politics? Come to Europe with your family, and let's scrape a living and study together as we've always wanted to do!"

Thomas smiled and shook his head.

"It sounds attractive. But, no, my dear friend. It's all very well for you; you're a wanderer who doesn't owe anything to any country. For me, it's different. I'm an Englishman, and my country needs me. Because a ship is sinking is no reason to desert her. One should stay on board and try to bail out water as long as possible."

"So you're going to stay on the English ship until she sinks?"

"Or swims!" replied Thomas. "But goodness me, Erasmus! We've got better things than politics to talk about when our time together is so short!"

Skilfully Thomas changed the subject. His heart was full of sadness and anxiety for the future of his beloved country, but he made a great effort to seem as cheerful as usual.

6

PORTRAIT OF A FAMILY

IN 1520, THOMAS MORE was forty-two, and thirty years
had passed since his boyish tricks had entertained the
guests at Lambeth Palace. Now Thomas was an important person. He had several very responsible posts at
court, and, the following year, in recognition of all his
hard work, he was to be given the right to call himself
"Sir Thomas" instead of plain "Mr. More".

Yet Thomas had changed very little in those thirty years. His light brown hair was still thick and rich in color. His cheeks were pink, and his blue-gray eyes still sparkled merrily. He had never grown very tall. As he walked, he had the habit of hitching one shoulder higher than the other, so that his cloak fell rather untidily to one side. Thomas never gave a thought to his appearance. There were far more interesting things to absorb him.

Thomas was always busy, but he did not neglect his home life and his family. He spent as much time with them as possible, sharing their joys and their sorrows, their everyday routines and their great occasions.

The second of July 1521 was a very great occasion for the Mores, so Thomas treated himself to a whole holiday. His eldest daughter, sixteen-year-old Margaret, was being married to William Roper, a lawyer of twenty-three.

The ceremony took place in the parish church at Bucklersbury. Afterward, when the guests had thrown ears of ripe wheat over the couple as a sign that they hoped there would be many children, they returned to the More house for the wedding feast.

Thomas loved a homely gathering of this sort, and he was a perfect host. He moved about from one guest to another, greeting each one as though he were the particular person he wanted to see.

"Congratulations, Sir Thomas, on your latest promotion!" called one of the guests. "Undertreasurer of

England! My goodness, that must keep you occupied! And how do you like having 'Sir' in front of your name?"

"To tell you the truth, it's my wife who enjoys the title!" smiled Thomas. "As to being occupied, yes, I certainly am!"

"Ah, but I'm sure you still find time to be with King Henry. You're such a favorite of his! And I expect His Grace tells you all his secrets?" asked the guest, who was rather inquisitive. He pulled Thomas closer and whispered confidentially, "They say that this conference between France and Spain next month is only a blind and that as soon as England has finished being peacemaker between the two, she's going to join Spain in a war against France. Is that true?"

"You'd better ask the king!" replied Thomas, refusing, as always, to be drawn into gossip. The guest looked very disappointed.

"Oh, come, Sir Thomas, you needn't be so secretive! You're among friends."

"Indeed, yes. And enjoying their company very much!" said Thomas cheerily. He excused himself and moved away.

On the other side of the room his daughter Margaret was looking very pretty and excited, though a little nervous, too. He went across to her.

"Dear Father, I'm terribly happy", she whispered. "I love my William so much!"

"He's a good man, my dear. He'll make you a fine husband."

"Oh, I know! Only—I'm a bit worried about him", Margaret frowned anxiously. "Poor Will, he's prayed and fasted so much in preparation for our marriage that he seems to have worn himself out and got quite confused in his mind. Father, I believe he's turning away from our Catholic faith!"

"I realize that. He's spoken to me, too", said Thomas gently. "But you mustn't be disturbed, dearest. At heart, William holds the faith very strongly. If he does slip away, I feel sure it won't be for long. Meanwhile I'll talk with him, and you pray for him, Meg. Everything will be all right. Now, here comes your brother, looking very important! Well, young John, what is it?"

"Please, Father, there's an old beggar outside. He wanted to know if this was the home of Sir Thomas, who always helped anyone in trouble. He says he must see you. But you're not seeing people today, are you?"

"That's for Margaret to decide. It's her day", replied Thomas. "Well, Meg? What are we to do about this poor old fellow?"

"He needs you, Father", said Margaret.

Thomas smiled approvingly.

"Good girl! Now, John, you must take my place and look after our guests. Good-bye for the present, little Margaret. God bless you!"

Thomas kissed his daughter and slipped away from the wedding feast. Then his holiday was over as he went to help a troubled old man who would never be able to pay him anything for his services.

Thomas' children were almost grown up by this time. A few years later, all the girls were married, including his stepdaughter, Alice, and an adopted daughter named Margaret Gigs. John More was engaged, and his fifteen-year-old fiancée had come to live with the Mores.

The children did not move away from home after they married. In those times private houses were very large, and it was customary for young couples to continue living with their parents.

Thomas realized that the city would be no place to bring up his future grandchildren. So he built a beautiful mansion at Chelsea, a village on the Thames about two miles upriver from London. It was a lovely situation, and all the family were delighted with their new home.

In 1527, the great Dutch painter Hans Holbein was visiting England. During the spring he went to stay with the Mores at Chelsea.

He arrived on a feast day, which was a public holiday, but, holiday or not, Thomas had work to do. So, for a while, Holbein was entertained by Thomas' daughters.

First they showed him the schoolroom, where, even though they were married, the young Mores still continued with their lessons. In those days it was unusual for girls to be taught much more than how to read, write, and sew, but Thomas believed that all young people should have a good education. His own children had become remarkable scholars, and Mr. Holbein was quite amazed to hear the girls carrying on a learned discussion in Latin.

Afterward, as a change from school subjects, they took him around the beautiful house. They showed him the museum, where Thomas had a large collection of fascinating objects. A piece of clear yellow amber with a fly in it was pointed out as Thomas' favorite piece.

Then the visitor was taken outside and shown Thomas' miniature zoo. Thomas loved animals of all kinds. He kept rabbits, badgers, squirrels, deer, and even a cunning little monkey.

"Now, Mr. Holbein, it's time for Margaret and me to do some visiting", said Margaret Roper, nodding toward her adopted sister. "Margaret's husband, John Clement, is the court physician now. Margaret is a clever doctor too, so she looks after the sick people in the village."

"I also distribute the money that our father gives me for the poor", added Margaret Clement. "Our father is very generous."

"He is! He has established a home near here for all our old retired servants. I'm in charge of that", said Margaret Roper. "We shall not be gone long, Mr. Holbein. Meanwhile, why don't you go and rest under the mulberry tree on the lawn? You'll probably find our grandfather there. He'll amuse you with the story of how he surprised all of us by getting married for the fourth time when he was over seventy!"

"Oh, I must hear about that!" laughed Holbein before going off to find Sir John More, who had indeed grown into a very entertaining old man.

Holbein and Sir John were still chuckling away

together when Thomas appeared. He was surrounded by his children, who clung affectionately to him, and fat little Dame Alice trotted along by his side.

Thomas greeted his guest warmly; then they all went in to dinner.

Holbein had a good appetite, and he enjoyed the excellent food that Dame Alice had provided. But he noticed that Thomas himself ate very little and drank water instead of wine.

At the beginning of the meal there was no talking. Instead, Margaret Clement read aloud from the New Testament. Then, at a signal from Thomas, she ate her dinner while the others discussed what had been read. Again Holbein was astonished at the intelligence of the well-educated young Mores.

When Thomas considered that there had been enough solemn talk, he sent for the resident comedian (one was employed by all rich people in those days), and the meal ended with laughter. It was very plain that Thomas, his father, and his whole family liked to have a lot of fun.

After dinner, Holbein suggested making a start on the family portrait of the Mores that he was going to paint. But Thomas thought his guest must be too tired to begin work that day. Instead, he offered to show him the New Building, the part of his property that was his special pride.

The New Building was a short distance away from the house in a quiet part of the garden. It consisted of a library, a gallery, and a chapel. Thomas explained that he had had this place built for himself in order to get away from his large family once in a while!

Holbein admired Thomas' valuable books and pictures. But what impressed him even more than the treasures was the wonderful atmosphere of peace.

"I use this place often", said Thomas, after they had knelt for a few minutes in the chapel. "I do all my writing and studying here in the library, and, if I have anything on my mind, I come here and ask God's help. God has been very good to me, Mr. Holbein. I remember when Margaret had the sweating sickness, and the doctors had almost given up hope. I was in the chapel here, begging God to spare her life, and he put into my head a treatment that the doctors hadn't even thought of."

"It cured her? How miraculous!" exclaimed Holbein. "How tremendously grateful you must have been!"

"Grateful? Mr. Holbein, if my dearest Meg had died, I should have retired from public life and never had anything to do with the world again!" declared Thomas, and Holbein realized just how devoted he was to his eldest daughter.

After they had examined the New Building, Thomas excused himself because he still had work to do. Holbein went out to enjoy the lovely garden that stretched down to the riverbank.

He left the lawns and strolled through a part of the garden that had been divided up into tiny plots. He knew that each plot belonged to one of the servants, and he saw some of them working away at their flower beds or rows of vegetables. Thomas took a great interest in his servants. He had them taught gardening, music, and other hobbies so that they should not idle away their leisure and run the risk of falling into all sorts of temptations.

Suddenly Holbein realized that he had wandered too far. He was surrounded by paved yards and sheds and had lost himself completely. Then he saw a young woman hanging out some clothing to dry, and he went to ask his way.

"Excuse me, my girl. Oh, it's Mistress Roper! I do beg your pardon . . ." Holbein stopped short. He was staring in amazement at the garment in Margaret's hands. It was so coarse and hairy that it looked almost like the skin of a monkey. "My goodness! Forgive me, but whatever is that, Mistress Roper?"

Margaret blushed. Then she made a little face and smiled.

"Well, Mr. Holbein, since you've caught me in the act I'd better explain. I'm washing my father's shirt. He doesn't let anyone do it but me, because he doesn't like people to know that he wears it."

"You mean to say he wears *that* thing next to his skin?" cried Holbein in dismay.

"Yes. He's been wearing a hair shirt like this ever since he was a young man. It's a sort of permanent penance."

"Good heavens! What wonderful endurance to bear a penance like that for years on end!"

"My father *is* wonderful", said Margaret, and her eyes shone. "Father's so good and kind. And so strong. Nobody could ever make him change his mind if he decided to do something that he believed was right. Yet he's full of fun, as you saw at dinner. Did he show you his New Building? He prays there for hours, sometimes most of the night. And on Fridays, or special feast days, when he can get away from court, he spends all day there, praying and meditating."

"Perhaps that's why he seems so at peace", suggested Holbein.

"Of course!" replied Margaret. "You see, he has complete trust in God."

The shirt had been pegged on the clothesline now, and Margaret accompanied Holbein back to the gardens. As they walked, she told him of the terrible time when her husband, William Roper, had fallen away from the faith. In England at that period, to deny the Catholic faith and support the false doctrines of the Lutheran heretics was regarded as a real crime. A man who became a heretic was liable to be put to death, or at least have all his possessions confiscated and himself and his relations disgraced forever. So William Roper had put the whole More family into great danger by his action.

"He was so miserable, poor Will, for the devil had hold of him", said Margaret. "Father was wonderful, of course. As a rule, heresy is the one thing that can make him really angry. Or, not so much heresy as heretics who lead astray simple folk who can't think much for themselves. But Father never once lost patience with William. He used to reason with him for hours at a time. But in the end he said to me, 'It's no good, Meg. I can't do anything. We'll just have to bring son Roper back to the faith with our prayers.' And so we did! Now I think Will is the best Catholic of us all. Except, of course, my father."

Margaret smiled to herself as she thought about the father she loved so much. Then she turned to Holbein again.

"Now I'm afraid I must desert you for the second time! We're a highly organized household, as I expect you've noticed, and I have my jobs to do. Good-bye for the present."

They parted, and Holbein amused himself happily for the rest of the afternoon.

The whole family came together again at supper. Afterward they had an enjoyable little singsong, accompanying themselves on the lute and the harp. From Thomas' happy expression it was clear that to spend a homely evening with his loved ones was his greatest pleasure.

"But I'm afraid it's bedtime now", he announced at last. There was a loud groan from everyone.

"Oh, Father! Just a few more minutes!"

"No, indeed! If you don't get your sleep, none of you will be up in the morning. And you won't get to heaven in featherbeds, you know!" he laughed, firmly putting an end to the protests.

Lanterns were brought, and a little procession walked from the house to the chapel in the New Building, where the servants were already waiting.

Thomas led the simple night prayers, and he spoke to God as though he could truly sense his presence all around. Holbein noticed that Thomas mentioned by name all the sick people in the village and that he gave thanks for a very great favor. Perhaps he meant son-in-law Roper's return to the Church? Holbein did not know. But he did know that he, himself, was already feeling the peace and happiness of that loving, united More family.

Before he got into bed Holbein glanced out of the window. There was still a glimmer of light from the New Building, where Thomas worked and prayed far into the night.

7

THE KING'S BUSINESS

MANY VISITORS came to Chelsea besides Hans Holbein. One evening, quite unexpectedly, Henry VIII himself arrived.

Thomas treated his king just like any other guest. He showed him around the house and garden, gave him a good family dinner, and, when he left, begged him sincerely to come again. Henry must have enjoyed himself, for he did often come again. The More family felt thrilled as they watched him strolling arm in arm with their father.

"His Grace chats away as though you were his brother!" declared William Roper triumphantly. "You certainly are his favorite!"

"Perhaps. But that doesn't count for very much", Thomas replied soberly. "I'm quite sure that if the king could win just one castle in France by chopping off my head, he'd do so without any hesitation!"

"Father! How terrible!" exclaimed Roper. "It's true; both His Grace, the king, and the lord chancellor, Cardinal Wolsey, *are* very ambitious. They plot against their own allies, and they rush into one war after another, which we poor English people have to pay for. It's dreadful to watch England become the most unpopular country in Europe. Father, can't you use your influence?"

"I? My son, I may be one of the chief officials in the kingdom, but I have as little real influence with His Grace as the woman who washes his shirts!" replied Thomas sadly. What William Roper had said was true. Henry VIII and Cardinal Wolsey could think of nothing but the power and glory they wanted for themselves. Thomas knew that his country was being ruined by the selfishness of two men. And there was nothing he could do except stay in his job and pray that he might have the chance to help save England.

In 1523, Thomas had the honor of being made speaker, or leader, of the House of Commons. He immediately

did the members of Parliament a great service. He persuaded Henry VIII to promise that the members could
say anything they liked while they were in the Parliament
chamber without fear of getting themselves into trouble.
Previously, there had been no such thing as freedom of
speech for them.

Thomas had a hard task as speaker. The members of
Parliament were highly indignant, and with reason.
Henry VIII wanted them to pass a tax that would be
equal to one-fifth of everything each person in England
possessed! Thomas needed all his tact and patience to
keep the members in order. Then, when at last the
members agreed to pass a tax equal to only about half of
what the king demanded, it was poor Thomas who got
the blame.

"*Half!*" exploded Cardinal Wolsey, who wanted the
money for his wars as much as Henry did. "Upon my
word, Mr. More, I wish you'd been in Rome when I
made you speaker!"

"So do I, my lord! I'd love to see Rome", replied
Thomas calmly, and then he went on to talk of something quite different. He had handled both the members
of Parliament and the cardinal with great skill and had
smoothed over a difficult situation. But there were to be
many other far more serious situations that Thomas
would have to face.

Life at court was becoming increasingly hard for Thomas to bear. Day after day he had to watch the wicked,
selfish behavior of Henry VIII and Wolsey. A weaker-

minded man would have given up long ago and resigned his job. But Thomas knew that God's way was not always the easiest way and that it was his duty to remain at court.

One summer evening, the king made another unexpected visit to Chelsea. It was clear that he had something on his mind, and, after he had been strolling on the lawn with Thomas for a while, he said confidentially, "Mr. More, you're my very good friend, and I'm going to let you in on a secret. I'm in love! Oh, it's wonderful. I feel like a boy again! I mean to marry her as soon as possible, my adorable little Anne Boleyn!"

For a moment Thomas felt too horrified to speak. Anne Boleyn was one of the queen's ladies-in-waiting. She was an unpleasant, spiteful woman, not even intelligent or pretty. But she had been brought up in the French court, so perhaps her foreign ways had attracted Henry VIII.

"And what about Queen Catherine?" asked Thomas. He was very devoted to this gentle, gracious Spanish lady.

"I shall divorce her", said the king. "We have nothing in common, and it's getting on my nerves. It might have been different if we'd had a son. I *must* have a son to succeed me as king, but no sons come. I believe it's a judgment on me for having married Catherine. Being my brother's widow, she was really a sort of relation, and I don't believe it was right for us to marry. Besides, as Wolsey himself pointed out, think how convenient it would be for me to marry Anne, now that we're trying to get on good terms with the French again! And, if I do divorce Catherine, it'll serve those treacherous Spaniards right!"

Thomas had been listening in dismay. Now he spoke out.

"Your Grace, I'm sure you need have no doubts about your marriage to Queen Catherine. Pope Julius II gave you permission to marry."

"Ah, but he might have made a mistake, might he not?" Henry replied. "There are parts of the Bible that more or less say a man can divorce his wife under some circumstances. Let's get a Bible, and I'll show you."

"Please, Your Grace, I'd prefer to have nothing to do with this matter!" said Thomas. The king stared.

"What? But I was sure you would be on my side! In your book *Utopia* the people were allowed divorce!"

"My Utopians were not Christians like us, with Christ's laws to obey! If it please Your Grace, I beg you to leave me out of this", insisted Thomas bravely. Henry VIII seemed about to fly into a rage. Then he shrugged.

"Well, we won't say any more now. But you needn't imagine you can get out of giving me an answer, Mr. More! I shall bring up this matter again, so read all the parts of the Holy Scriptures that have anything to do with marriage and discuss the whole question with your learned friends. I'm *sure* I'm free to marry Anne Boleyn, and you'll see in the end I'm right!"

Henry VIII had a convenient conscience that allowed him to believe anything he wanted to believe. But Thomas was stricter with himself. Even though he was the king's loyal servant, he knew that he would never be able to agree that Henry's divorce plans were right. He was in a very difficult position. That evening Thomas spent a long time in his chapel, praying for God's help in the troubles he saw ahead.

The following day Thomas set off with the king for a trip to Oxford and Cambridge. It was pleasant for Thomas to be in Oxford again and see many of his learned friends, who seldom came to London. Thomas could always make the best of life, so he enjoyed his stay in spite of his anxieties.

Henry VIII was visiting the university towns in order to ask the various professors and scholars for their opinion about his marriage. Had it really been lawful for him to marry Catherine, or had Pope Julius made a mistake in granting him that permission? Surely there were passages in the Bible that said quite definitely that no man might marry his brother's widow? These tricky questions had to be settled before Henry could get his divorce.

Henry felt very resentful against Thomas for refusing to help him. But, for a while, he left Thomas alone. Certainly Thomas needed all his time to get through his normal work.

"What keeps you so busy, husband? We barely see you these days", complained Dame Alice.

"I'm helping Cardinal Wolsey look after England's affairs abroad", explained Thomas. "We're working out a new peace treaty with France."

"Well, I don't expect that'll last long!" declared Dame Alice. "Wars, wars! And now there's a rumor that the cardinal plans to join us with those horrid French in a war against the Spanish, who used to be our friends! The cardinal wants to keep in with the French only because they have influence with the Pope. He means to be pope himself one day. Even I know that!"

"You seem to know a lot, dear", said Thomas, who refused to gossip even with his wife. "Admittedly, my Lord Wolsey's plans *are* very complicated. The trouble is, the more complicated a plan, the more easily it can go wrong."

Cardinal Wolsey's schemes did soon go very wrong indeed. As a result, Thomas' whole future was changed.

One day in May 1527, Thomas reported as usual to the king. Henry VIII was in a great state of excitement.

"Something frightful has happened!" he cried. "Those undisciplined Spanish soldiers have invaded Rome. They've behaved like barbarians, and they've captured Pope Clement himself! The Spanish emperor is holding him prisoner."

"*What!* But doesn't the emperor realize that the pope is Christ's own representative here on earth?" Thomas exclaimed. Henry waved his hand impatiently.

"That's not the point! The thing is, I particularly wanted Pope Clement's help to get my divorce from

Catherine. But he's not likely to grant me the divorce so long as he's in the power of the Spanish emperor— Catherine's own nephew!"

"I daresay you're right", said Thomas shortly. He felt very tired of wars and politics and plots, and this news of the Pope's capture had shocked him terribly.

A few weeks later, Cardinal Wolsey and Thomas went to Amiens, France, for the signing of the peace treaty between France and England. The French had planned many celebrations to mark this great event. There were banquets and other extravagant entertainments for the English ambassadors and the army of richly dressed officials and servants who accompanied proud Cardinal Wolsey wherever he went. Thomas had to play his part— be polite to his hosts and pretend that he was enjoying himself. But, as always, he felt very thankful to leave the magnificence behind and return to his own simple ways at home.

He had barely arrived back in London when again Henry VIII asked for Thomas' opinion about his marriage and his chances of divorce. Again Thomas refused to answer. He would not even say why he refused. This was a matter that each person had to think out and decide for himself. Thomas was not going to influence anybody by stating his own views.

It needed tremendous willpower to remain silent about something so very important. Everyone was discussing the king's divorce, but never once would Thomas allow himself to do so. Even to his close friend

Bishop Fisher of Rochester, the only English bishop strong-minded enough to insist that the divorce would be wrong, Thomas refused to confide his opinion. Yet he felt very concerned.

"Oh, Son! If three things could happen, I'd willingly be put into a sack and thrown into the River Thames!" he declared one evening to William Roper as they strolled along the riverbank at Chelsea.

"What three things are those?" asked William Roper.

"First, that instead of being at war the world might be at peace. Second, that the Church might be completely united and free from these terrible heresies. And third, that this business of the king's marriage might be settled according to God's will."

"Well, it looks as though the marriage business might soon be settled, if not according to God's will!" said Roper. "The Pope has appointed Cardinal Wolsey and an Italian cardinal to go into the whole matter and decide whether the king's marriage to Catherine was ever a true marriage or not. It's ridiculous! With Wolsey absolutely on the king's side, everyone knows what the result of this 'trial' will be before it even begins! I can't think why the Pope doesn't make his own decision without appointing legates to decide for him!"

"The point is, Pope Clement doesn't want to be involved." said Thomas, sadly. Then, for his son-in-law's sake, he made a great effort to be cheerful. There was no point in being distressed over something they could do nothing about.

In May 1529, Henry VIII received a formal notice to appear before Cardinal Wolsey and the other papal legate. He was to explain to them how he came to be married to his brother's widow. Then they would decide whether or not his marriage had ever been a true marriage in the sight of God.

Friends of poor, courageous Queen Catherine, such as Thomas and Bishop Fisher, waited with heavy hearts to hear the result of this "trial". Then a sudden crisis abroad drew Thomas' thoughts to other matters.

It was a hot afternoon toward the end of June 1529 when Thomas received an urgent message from Henry VIII. He found Henry pacing about his office in a wild rage.

"They've been scheming behind our backs again!" cried Henry. "I've been made a fool of, and it's all Wolsey's fault!"

"Whom do you mean by 'they', Your Grace?"

"France and Spain, of course! We heard weeks ago that they were planning a meeting at Cambrai to arrange peace between themselves without letting England know. That's just the sort of trick France would play on her ally! But Wolsey swore this was only a rumor—'an invention of the enemy', he said. Invention, bah! They're at Cambrai now! Wolsey's been too clever by far. His foreign schemes have won us nothing but the hatred of Europe!"

Henry VIII threw a handful of documents onto the floor and stamped on them. Thomas said quietly, "The point is, what's to be done now to make the best of things?"

"I was coming to that. An English envoy will have to go to Cambrai at once, or France and Spain will have come to an agreement, and England won't get any benefit from it. Wolsey can't go; he's done enough damage already. Besides, he's busy settling my divorce business, so I'm sending you and the bishop of London. You've both had plenty of experience on these missions, so I'll expect you to get a good bargain for England."

"We'll do our best, Your Grace", said Thomas, resigning himself to yet another difficult and tedious mission. "At any rate, let us hope this meeting at Cambrai means permanent peace at last!"

"No thanks to Wolsey if it does!" growled Henry VIII.

It was not at all pleasant to ride on horseback through dusty France in midsummer. The ambassadors arrived exhausted. However, Thomas never let his work suffer just because he was tired. He behaved with such tact and skill during the meetings between the French, Spanish, and English that when the peace treaty was finally drawn up he had won far more benefits for England than even Henry VIII could have expected.

While Thomas and the bishop of London were in Cambrai, important news arrived. Henry VIII had failed to get his divorce. The Italian cardinal had closed the court for the summer vacation without making any decision about the king's marriage.

"He had instructions from Pope Clement, that's plain!" said the bishop to Thomas. "Everyone knows that the court won't reopen. Oh, Mr. More, I dread to think what King Henry will do to revenge himself against the Pope for not helping him get his divorce!"

"I shouldn't think Cardinal Wolsey will be any too popular with His Grace now, either!" remarked Thomas.

"No, indeed! The rumor goes that it's only a matter of time before Wolsey is dismissed. Moreover, King Henry seems determined to break with tradition and have a layman instead of a priest for his next lord chancellor."

The bishop paused and looked closely at Thomas.

"I can guess whom His Grace is likely to appoint. How would you feel about being lord chancellor of England, Mr. More?"

Thomas grinned suddenly.

"As my wife would tell you, I've no ambition! But that's hardly the point. I am the king's servant, and if he wants me to be lord chancellor, I shall not have much choice in the matter. Besides, I'd gladly do anything that might help England."

"Well, whoever he is, the next lord chancellor will need all our prayers!" declared the bishop. "To be chancellor of England during troubled times like these, and under such a king as His Grace, Henry VIII, is going to be a hard task."

"It is", said Thomas. Then his eyes twinkled merrily

as he thought again of Dame Alice. "But imagine, my lord, how the new chancellor's wife will love her important position! That should make up for a lot!"

8

LORD CHANCELLOR

I N THE LATE FALL of 1529, Cardinal Wolsey was dismissed from his post as lord chancellor.

Thomas had already decided to take over the job if it were offered to him. His sense of duty was so strict that he knew he must do whatever the king wished, provided it was not something wrong. Certainly he would have no fun as lord chancellor. He would have even less time to himself, and he would probably make many dangerous enemies, as men in high position were almost bound to do. But those would be selfish reasons for refusing responsibility, and Thomas thought things out in his completely unselfish way. He loved his king and his country, and he meant to do his best for them, no matter what it cost.

One October day, soon after Wolsey's dismissal, Thomas was sent for by the king. He noticed that the lord chancellor's badge of office was lying on Henry's desk.

"Well, we've got rid of Wolsey at last", said Henry VIII. "I've had enough of priests, and I'm not going to have any more of them interfering in state matters. You've proved yourself to be competent and loyal, Mr. More, so I've decided to make you my new lord chancellor."

"You do me a great honor," replied Thomas, "though, if a more suitable man can be found . . ."

"If there were a more suitable man, I shouldn't be asking you!" snapped Henry. "I want *you* for chancellor, Mr. More!"

"In that case, I shall be glad to accept", Thomas answered.

There was no more hope that something might happen to prevent his having to undertake this tremendous task. Thomas was to be the leading citizen of England, with the heaviest responsibility for its welfare.

The day that he was made lord chancellor of England might have been Thomas More's great day. But worldly success meant nothing to him, and he felt no triumph. He knew that the time would come when he would have to show how strongly he disapproved of much of Henry VIII's behavior. He knew that sooner or later there would be serious disagreement between himself and his strong-willed king. The future looked black to Thomas as he walked out of the palace carrying the chancellor's badge.

Thomas was well liked in England, so everyone was pleased to hear of his great promotion. Dame Alice, of course, was highly delighted. She thoroughly enjoyed being the first lady in England and buying herself many nice dresses to suit her position.

Thomas himself did not change any of his ways. He refused to show his power, as Cardinal Wolsey had done, by giving huge banquets or by surrounding himself with servants. Visitors to Chelsea found everything exactly as before. The meals were still fairly plain, but enjoyable. The servants were the same simple villagers who knew that, though their master was such an important person, they could still take their troubles to him.

The English had grown used to the idea that officials were proud, unfriendly folk. But they soon realized that there was nothing proud or unfriendly about Sir Thomas More. When he was walking to his office in the law courts, with his secretaries behind and his official cross-bearer in front, Thomas would often halt the little procession in order to have a friendly chat with someone. And when he passed through the court where Sir John More, the judge, was presiding, it was very usual to see Thomas go down on his knees for his elderly father's blessing.

One Sunday morning, when the whole More household was at Mass, the Duke of Norfolk arrived with a
message for Thomas from the king. The little Chelsea
parish church was packed tight, and at first the duke
could see no sign of Thomas. When he did catch sight
of him, he gasped. Thomas, the lord chancellor of England, was singing in the choir among the local trades-
men! The duke considered Thomas' behavior most
undignified. As soon as Mass was over, he told him so.

"Really, Mr. More! I don't think the king would be at
all pleased to know that his lord chancellor was dressed
in a surplice and singing away like a common choirboy!"

Thomas laughed loudly at this rebuke.

"I'm quite sure my lord, the king, wouldn't object to
my paying homage to my king's Lord!" he replied cheerily. Thomas saw no reason to give himself airs just because he had an important job to do.

After Thomas had been lord chancellor for a while,
Henry VIII sent for him.

"Well, Mr. More, you've had time to get adjusted to
your new job", he said briskly. "And now I'm going to
ask you a question you've heard before. What's your real
opinion about my marriage? Don't you agree that I
never was and never could be truly married to Catherine,
my own sister-in-law? And that Pope Julius II should
never have given us permission to marry because this
was something beyond even a pope's power to decide?
Come on, now, be frank! What do you say?"

"What I've always said, Your Grace", answered Thomas. "I'm extremely sorry that I can't cooperate with you in this matter. But it's something for each person's own conscience to decide."

"Conscience! Bah!" retorted Henry. "Other people's consciences haven't prevented them from giving me a straight answer. I don't know why you should be such an exception!"

Thomas said nothing but let the king boil and fume.

"Plenty of men have given me their opinions without all this fuss", Henry repeated. "But it's not their opinions I want. It's yours, my good friend! We are good friends, aren't we? And haven't I been generous to you all these years you've been in my service?"

"You have, indeed", agreed Thomas. The king was trying to get what he wanted by making him feel ungrateful. But Thomas would not be bullied, as the king soon realized.

"Very well, Mr. More. Since you're determined to be stubborn, I'll get other men to help me with my divorce. You can concentrate on your chancellor's duties", he said resentfully. "Anyway, one thing's certain. The people can be sure of justice from a chancellor with such a hardworking conscience as yours!"

Henry VIII was right. The English people did have great confidence in their new lord chancellor. Thomas' strict sense of right and wrong made him extremely popular among the ordinary people, who often suffered because of the wickedness of those in authority. However, some of Thomas' friends and relatives were disappointed when they found there was nothing to be gained by knowing the chancellor well!

"Even the doorkeeper at Cardinal Wolsey's palace profited more than any of us do", grumbled one of Thomas' sons-in-law. "Wolsey's doorkeeper could always earn plenty of tips by letting people in to see the cardinal. But not a soul offers *us* money to get to see you, Father. You're always willing to see anyone!"

"And is it such a bad thing to be willing to see anyone?" smiled Thomas.

"No, of course not, sir. It's most admirable. But it's not very profitable for us!"

"My dear son, I will help you in any way I can. But any suggestion of unfair dealing I will not tolerate!" declared Thomas firmly. "Why, if I had to try a case between my father and the devil himself, I'd settle in favor of the devil if right were on his side!"

Thomas was never faced with quite such a tricky situation. But one day he did have to settle a dispute between his wife and an old woman.

A stray dog had been found at Chelsea, and Dame Alice had adopted it. She grew extremely fond of her little pet, and, when an old village woman came to claim it, she refused to give it up.

"I won't! I've looked after him, and now he's mine!" she declared.

"He's mine, madam!" wailed the old woman. "Please, Sir Thomas, sir, he's my own little dog. Really he is!"

"Well, ladies, I think the dog himself had better decide this", said Thomas patiently. "Give him to me, Alice dear. Now I shall stand here with him, and each of you go to opposite ends of the room. When I say 'go', call the dog's name. Whichever of you he runs to shall keep him. Are you ready? Go!"

The two women shrieked the dog's name. He wriggled out of Thomas' arms and ran to the old villager.

"Well, that settles that", said Thomas. But Dame Alice looked so disappointed that he asked the old woman if she would consider selling the dog.

A few minutes later, Dame Alice was again cuddling her pet, the old woman had gone home with a pocketful of money, and both were delighted at the result of Thomas' wise handling of the affair.

Thomas enjoyed his work among the poor people. But there were also much less pleasant tasks that the lord chancellor had to attend to.

One of the most important and difficult of these tasks was to control the anti-Catholic heretics who were spreading their harmful doctrines through England. They had caused so many disturbances among the people that there was grave danger of civil war breaking out.

Another of the chancellor's duties was to receive foreign ambassadors and discuss politics with them. He also had to sit for hours in the king's council. And, as the king's personal representative, it was his job to deliver messages from the king to the members of Parliament.

The week after Thomas became lord chancellor, he had to accompany Henry VIII to an opening session of

Parliament. All through English history the opening of Parliament has been a very formal occasion. But the ceremony on November 3, 1529, was particularly grand because Henry VIII meant it to be a particularly important Parliament.

Thomas, wearing his magnificent official robes, stood beside the king's throne in the Parliament chamber and told the members why they had been ordered to meet.

"Gentlemen, for some time our good King Henry has been greatly shocked by the bad behavior of the clergy in England. Instead of being an example to us, they are the opposite. The monasteries have become luxurious palaces, and many of our priests are a disgrace to us. Therefore, gentlemen, on behalf of His Grace, our king, I have to tell you that you have been called together in order to pass laws that will reform the Church in England."

Thomas delivered his speech clearly and firmly. But he felt very uneasy. To reform the Church in England was indeed an excellent plan. But Thomas knew that Henry's ideas of reform were quite different from his own. He realized that Henry was not thinking of England's good. Henry simply wanted to spite the Pope, who had refused to grant his divorce. He could do nothing to the Pope himself, so he planned to get his revenge on the English bishops, the Pope's representatives in England. For Thomas the tragedy was that, even though he was the most important man in England, he could do nothing to prevent the headstrong king from carrying out his plans.

Henry VIII's first step was to demand a huge fine from the English clergy and to order them to accept him as "Sole Protector and Supreme Head of the Church and Clergy in England". The bishops objected, but they stood no chance against Henry. In February 1531, they gave him his title of protector, though they added the words "so far as the law of God allows".

"My goodness, husband, what a shocking thing!" exclaimed Dame Alice when she heard the news. "Can an ordinary king really meddle like this in Church matters?"

"His Grace doesn't consider himself an ordinary king!" Thomas replied.

Thomas felt horrified and distressed that Henry VIII should dare to put himself in authority over God's Church and God's ministers. He had tried to resign in protest, but the king refused angrily to accept his resignation. He and Thomas could never again be the close friends they had once been. Henry's greed had come between them.

Henry VIII continued his campaign against the bishops. Early in 1532 his friends in Parliament started a great attack on them. The bishops were accused of all manner of misdeeds, many of which were at least partly true. All of Thomas' sons-in-law were members of Parliament by this time, so Thomas waited anxiously for news of what was going on.

"The king says he's going to judge without prejudice

in this quarrel between Parliament and the bishops", reported William Roper. "His Grace without prejudice, indeed! Everyone knows that he's just waiting to seize the power of the English bishops for himself! Oh, Father, why did you let yourself become chancellor in terrible times like these?"

"Because it was my duty, Son. Why else? Don't you think I'd rather have stayed at home among the family and been merry with us all together?" replied Thomas. He smiled as he spoke, but his face was drawn and pale.

Thomas was no longer a boyish-looking man. He had suffered a sad loss in 1530, when his father died. Since then nobody had called him "young More" to distinguish him from the old judge. And, indeed, Thomas did not feel young any more, as he looked around at his five children and eleven grandchildren, and as he watched the affairs of his country go from bad to worse.

At last, on May 15, 1532, the English bishops gave in completely to Henry's VIII's bullying. They handed over to him all the authority of the Church in England. It was as though Henry VIII had declared himself pope of England.

The next morning Thomas arrived for his usual ten o'clock conference with the king. For once there was no hint of a smile on Thomas' face.

"A very good day to you!" greeted Henry VIII cheerfully. "And what's our business today?"

"If it please Your Grace, the business of my resignation. I must ask to be relieved of the chancellorship."

Henry turned crimson with rage. He knew quite well why Thomas wanted to resign, but he was not going to admit it.

"Relieved of the chancellorship? At a time like this?" he bellowed. "Here am I, my hands full of divorce matters, Church reform, and goodness knows what. And just when I need a loyal chancellor *you* ask to be relieved! *I'd* be very relieved if we heard no more of this nonsense!"

"I'm afraid we must", said Thomas quietly.

"I won't accept your resignation!"

"I'm sorry, Your Grace, but I must insist that you do."

Henry VIII gaped. Very few men ever had dared to stand up to him in this way.

"Why do you want to resign?" he asked sulkily.

"My health hasn't been good recently", Thomas answered. It was quite true. As a result of years of overwork and of sitting at his desk in an airless room, he had developed chronic bronchitis.

"Ah, yes, your health", the king nodded. Bad health was as good an excuse as any. He would have preferred Thomas More to remain in his service, but if Thomas was going to be difficult it was best that they should part on friendly terms.

"I shall be sorry to lose you, but of course your health comes first", said Henry, with a great show of kindness and generosity. He was already deciding whom to appoint as his next lord chancellor. Thomas More was no longer any use, and now suddenly Henry wanted him out of the way. "Well, Mr. More, I shall not forget all your hard work. Good-bye, my friend. I may take a little trip to Chelsea one of these days."

Henry VIII turned back to his desk.

Thomas glanced for the last time at the king he had watched grow up and whose loyal servant he would always be. Then he left the room. He was too wise not to realize the danger he was in. He had refused to take any part in Henry VIII's ambitious, evil schemes, and one day Henry would get his revenge.

Thomas went into the chapel to say a few prayers for his king and for himself. Then he walked slowly out of the palace into the spring sunshine. He was a ruined man, a nobody.

9

THE KING'S WRATH

BACK IN HIS LIBRARY at Chelsea, Thomas sat down to think out his position. He was out of work, he was sick, and soon he would also be quite poor.

Thomas could have lived in luxury for the rest of his life if he had acted like other officials and made himself rich while he was in power. But Thomas had never taken a penny more than his official salary. Most of that had been spent on the heavy expenses that a lord chancellor and father of a large family had to pay. Nearly all the rest Thomas gave away. He did not believe in keeping his money to himself when there was so much good to be done with it. So, when Thomas retired, he had only a small pension and the rents from various pieces of land.

Thomas finished working out his finances. Then he called the whole family for a conference.

"Well, my dears, it looks like dry bread for the lot of us!" he greeted them, smiling so cheerfully that no one could feel depressed. "I find there's only about a hundred pounds a year for all of us to live on. That includes the servants and the old people we take care of. So, children, I'm afraid from now on I'll have to ask each of you to help out."

"You're asking our children to *pay* for their keep?" wailed Dame Alice. "Oh, husband, what a shocking thing!"

"Not at all, Mother", said Margaret Roper quickly. "Father has done so much for us; it's only fair we should help now. I'm sure we'll all be glad to, won't we?"

"Of course!" chorused Thomas' children. He smiled tenderly at them.

"God bless you for your generosity! We're going to have to economize pretty strictly, you know. But we'll do it gradually. We'll begin by living on the standard of Lincoln's Inn, where the food was quite good, I remember. The next year we'll go down a grade to New Inn standard. Then the third year we'll go on to the really plain living that I got used to in my student days at Oxford. And if we find we can't afford to live even as simply as that, why, we'll just have to go round the streets singing for our supper!"

"Tilly-vally, tilly-vally, husband! The ex-lord chancellor begging! What a notion!" retorted Dame Alice, but the others laughed loudly at the idea. Then John More asked Thomas a question.

"Father, now that you've all the free time in the world, whatever will you do with yourself?"

Thomas smiled. "That's easy! I shall work at the studies I've had to neglect these past years. I shall read and write, and, in particular, I shall concentrate on something I've always wished I had time for—the fight against the heretics."

"Fight? You'll fight, Father?"

"With my pen, Son. When the heretics publish their clever articles, I'll answer them with articles of my own. I'll show how these Lutheran heretics misinterpret the laws that God made for us, and I'll try to explain the true Christian doctrines in words that the simplest people can understand."

Thomas' children listened enthusiastically. They felt even more anxious to help him now that they knew of the wonderful work he planned to do.

So the Chelsea household was reorganized. Thomas' children went to live in smaller, cheaper homes, and most of the big house was shut up. Positions were found for the servants who had to be dismissed. When at last everything had been arranged as well as possible, Thomas got down to work in his fight against the heretics.

These heretics were people who had broken away from the Catholic Church. They were followers of Martin Luther, a German monk who was around Thomas' own age.

Luther believed man was so evil that God's grace alone could save him. Prayers, penances, good works were all useless, declared Luther. He and his followers had many other beliefs quite contrary to the teaching of the Catholic Church. They did tremendous harm by spreading their false doctrines through Europe.

Sailors and merchants brought Lutheranism to England. It took such a hold that soon the country was threatened with civil war between the Lutherans and the Catholics. Laws were passed making heresy a very severe crime. But that was not enough. Wise and good men like Thomas knew that the only way to defeat the Lutherans was to give everyone a better understanding of the Catholic faith. So the bishops, priests, monks, and scholars set to work.

Thomas had already written many important articles against the heretics. In fact, he had done the Church such good service that the English bishops decided to reward him. They knew Thomas was now very poor, so they joined together to give him a large sum of money.

Thomas' friends urged him to accept this gift for his family if not for himself. But Thomas refused. His work against the Lutherans had been done for the love of God, not for a worldly reward. Besides, he was not going to risk having all his good work undone by giving his enemies a chance to say that he worked only for bribes.

The young Mores agreed loyally that their father did right to refuse the bishop's present. They often visited Thomas and Dame Alice in the empty, echoing great house, which was no longer the comfortable place it had been. On cold days they had to crouch over a miserable fire of bracken that they had gathered from the garden.

"My dears, I do hate not being able to give you so many of the things we used to take for granted", remarked Thomas during one of these visits. "Still, if life seems a little dreary and difficult just now, remember that no hardship can last long in this short life of ours. Anyway, think what a tiny thing the greatest suffering and sorrow must be compared with the tremendous, never-ending happiness in the next world!"

"Yes, I suppose that, compared to heaven, even martyrdom must seem a small thing", said Margaret Roper.

"Oh, no! Martyrdom is the greatest thing!" exclaimed Thomas. "Imagine the joy of giving the one you love most the thing he most longs for. That's the joy of martyrdom. More than anything, God wants us. And how more completely could we give ourselves to him than by sacrificing our very lives for him, as Christ sacrificed himself for us? What an honor to be chosen to follow like that in Christ's footsteps! No wonder that all through the ages martyrs have died rejoicing!"

"That's all very well," objected John More, "but what about the time *before* martyrdom? The months of imprisonment, loneliness, and even torture, perhaps?"

"That would be the hardest part," Thomas agreed, "but there would be God's grace to help us through. And the thought of that tremendous reward when we and our dear ones would be reunited in heaven!"

"Yes, Father; yes, indeed!" Thomas' listeners nodded and smiled. They felt extraordinarily cheered by his words. Thomas' cheerfulness and trust in God were a tremendous inspiration to his family during those difficult months after he had retired.

While Thomas was living quietly at Chelsea, Henry VIII had begun to show that he was indeed head of the Church in England, and he had broken completely with the Pope. In May 1533, the Archbishop of Canterbury weakly gave his consent to Henry's divorce from Catherine of Aragon. Already Henry and Anne Boleyn had been married secretly.

A magnificent ceremony was planned for the coronation of the new queen. Decorations went up in the main streets of London, and hundreds of pounds were distributed among the English poor to mark the great occasion. Every important person had to attend in order to pay his respects to the king's second wife.

But would Thomas attend? His acquaintances knew how loyal he had been to poor Catherine of Aragon. They feared he might stay away from Queen Anne's coronation with the excuse that he had no money for suitable clothes. If Thomas did that, he would be asking for trouble, they agreed.

Thomas' old friend the bishop of London, now bishop of Durham, and two other bishops tried to help him out. They gave Thomas a present of twenty pounds, asking him to spend it on a coronation robe and go with them to the ceremony. Thomas thanked them warmly for their generous gift, but on coronation day he stayed at home.

"What happened, Mr. More? Were you ill?" asked the bishop of Durham when next they met. "We were expecting you to come with us, but you never showed up!"

"So I didn't!" said Thomas with his mischievous grin. "You see, as I'd granted one of your requests and accepted your kind present, I thought you'd forgive me if I refused the other request and *didn't* come to the ceremony!"

"Well, I suppose you know that you angered the king and queen by your absence?" said the bishop gravely. "Queen Anne believes you insulted her deliberately! Don't you realize the dangerous position you've put yourself in?"

"Of course! But I realize your position, too!" Thomas replied. "Going to this coronation was equal to saying that you approved of the king's second marriage. And from now on you'll be expected to approve of everything he and his ministers do! Oh, I'd sooner have my danger than yours, my lord!"

Thomas' conscience was clear. Whatever happened, he was determined to stand by his ideas of right and wrong. This did not mean he was not afraid, because he was. He began to spend more time than ever in his chapel, begging God's grace to face whatever might be coming.

In January 1534, Henry VIII started his revenge against faithful Thomas. A document called a bill of attainder was made out, charging many Englishmen with treason because they had plotted against the king. Others were accused of having known about the plots and failing to report them. This was "misprision of treason", and one of the people accused was Thomas More.

Thomas knew that, if he were declared guilty of misprision of treason, he and his family would have all their possessions confiscated and would be in disgrace for the rest of their lives. More for his children's sake than for himself, Thomas used all his skill as a clever lawyer to prove that the charges against him were untrue. In the end Henry VIII had to order a special committee to investigate Thomas' case. He was ordered to appear before this committee at the House of Lords.

The day of the interview came, and Thomas set off with William Roper for company. Roper felt very anxious, but Thomas chatted quite coolly as they were rowed down the Thames toward London. Thomas was kept a long time in the House of Lords, but when at last he returned to the boat, he looked marvelously cheerful.

"How did you get on?" asked William Roper eagerly.

"Did you persuade the committee to take your name off the bill of attainder?"

"Why, no! I forgot all about the bill!"

"You *forgot* it?" cried Roper. "Something that concerns you so much, and us too, for your sake? Oh, Father! I was sure everything was all right, seeing you so merry!"

Thomas grinned. "I'm merry, Son, because I had an argument with the committee and thoroughly got the better of them! They brought up this wretched affair of the king's second marriage and wanted my opinion. I told them plainly that I'd hoped never to hear of the matter again. Then they began to threaten me and accuse me of fantastic things. I said to them, 'My lords, you may frighten children like this, but you won't frighten me!' Then I told them what I thought of them. In fact, I said so much I shall never be able to go back on it!"

Thomas chuckled to himself, but in his heart he was as worried as the rest of the family.

Several days passed. Then at last came the message that the Mores had longed for. Thomas' name had been taken off the bill of attainder. There had been so much argument in Parliament about Thomas' case that Henry VIII's advisers had persuaded him to drop the charges.

Thomas seemed strangely unexcited when he heard this news. Later he warned his eldest daughter, "Don't be too hopeful, Meg. I'm afraid trouble is only put off, not removed."

Thomas realized that he was still in grave danger. So did his friends. The Duke of Norfolk traveled down to Chelsea to tell Thomas how unwise he was in continuing to stand up against Henry VIII.

"I *beg* you to give way to His Grace a little, Mr. More. Remember that the anger of kings means death!"

"In that case, my lord, the only difference between us is that I shall die today and you tomorrow!" replied Thomas cheerfully. His courage and determination were amazing.

About two weeks later, the very thing happened that Thomas had dreaded. Henry had Parliament pass an "Act of Succession" stating that his and Anne Boleyn's children were to be the heirs of the English throne. The act also declared that Henry's first marriage had not been valid and that the Pope was not the head of the Church in England.

Henry VIII wanted to find out exactly who was on his side and who was not, so he ordered that everyone over the age of twenty-one had to sign an oath, swearing they agreed with everything in this Act of Succession.

Thomas could not agree. He knew that he would have to refuse the oath and take the consequences. He did not show his terrible fear. He just kept his beloved family with him as much as possible and tried very gently to prepare them for the worst. He reminded them continually that no matter what they might have to go through, the time would come when they would all join up in heaven and be "merry together" again.

On Low Sunday, April 12, 1534, Thomas and William Roper went up to London to hear a sermon at Saint Paul's Cathedral. Afterward they called on John and Margaret Clement, who were living in the Mores' old home at Bucklersbury, but their pleasant visit was interrupted. The news had spread that Sir Thomas was in town, and suddenly a court official arrived. He served Thomas with an order to report next day at Lambeth Palace, where he was to take his oath on the Act of Succession.

Thomas remained quite calm. He went straight home and spent his last evening at Chelsea, settling his affairs and saying good-bye to his family. Next morning he was up early. When Thomas had anything important to do, he always started his day with confession, Mass, and Holy Communion.

Very soon it was time to set out. He would not let the family see him off at the landing stage, as they usually did. When they tried to follow him, he shut the garden gate quickly behind him. In silence he walked to the boat with William Roper and the four servants who were going to row them downriver to Lambeth. Thomas' normally happy face was full of sorrow. He knew he was saying good-bye to his family, his home, and everything he loved most in life.

They rowed some distance without saying a word. Then Thomas turned to William Roper.

"Son, I thank God the battle is won!" he declared.

"I'm glad", replied Roper, though he did not

understand what Thomas meant. He did not realize the terrible struggle that had been going on inside Thomas. It would have been so easy for Thomas to give way and agree to anything that Henry VIII wanted him to agree to. But Thomas' conscience had said no, and conscience had won.

At last they arrived at Lambeth Palace, where Thomas had been so happy when he was a boy. He said good-bye to William Roper and sent an encouraging message back to the family at Chelsea. Then he went to face the beginning of his ordeal.

The king's councilors sat in a solemn row. Among them were Archbishop Cranmer of Canterbury and the king's secretary, Thomas Cromwell.

Thomas was shown a copy of the Act of Succession. He read it very carefully. Then he was shown the oath and told he must sign it. Thomas replied that he could not.

"And why not, Mr. More?" demanded Archbishop Cranmer.

"Because I don't agree to it. I'll certainly agree that the children of King Henry and Queen Anne are to inherit the English throne. But this oath makes me agree to other things as well. I can't sign it."

Cromwell snorted angrily and ordered Thomas to be shown the names of those who had already signed the oath.

"None of these people has objected, Mr. More. And they're all excellent men."

"Maybe. And if they sign, that's their business," said Thomas, "but I'm not going to!"

"Why not?"

"I'd prefer not to say."

The councilors whispered together for a moment. Then Thomas was ordered to go and wait in the garden.

The sun was very hot. It made Thomas feel weak and tired, so he went and sat in the shade of a ruined wing of the palace, where he was not likely to be disturbed.

Through the broken window he saw that the courtyard was full of men who, like himself, had been called to take their oath that day. They were all members of the clergy, and they seemed extremely cheerful, as though having to swear against the laws of their Church meant nothing to them. Thomas felt even more sad and lonely as he watched them.

He did not have long to rest before the councilors sent for him again.

"Well, Mr. More, have you thought over this matter of the oath?" asked Archbishop Cranmer.

"Yes, my lord," said Thomas bravely, "and I repeat that I cannot sign an oath agreeing to everything stated in this Act of Succession."

"You must obey the orders of your king!"

"Before anything I must obey my conscience", Thomas insisted. Then another councilor spoke.

"Mr. More, surely your conscience must be mistaken if it makes you defy all the wise men in the king's council?"

"Sir, which is it more important to obey—the council of an ordinary king or the general council of Christ's own Church?" challenged Thomas. The man flushed and did not answer.

Then Cromwell began to bully Thomas. Thomas was exhausted by this time, but nothing could break his spirit. He would not give in, and at last he was dismissed. But he was not allowed to go home. He was taken to the house of one of the councilors and told he must stay there without seeing anybody until Henry VIII had decided what should be done with him.

Thomas waited in suspense for four days. Then he heard that he was to be moved to the Tower of London. He pictured the fearsome jail where his own father had once been locked up. He knew that few prisoners came out of the Tower alive, except to take their last walk to their execution. He said a silent prayer. Then, with one of his customary little jokes, he told his jailer that he was quite ready to go.

IO

PRISONER IN THE TOWER

Thomas' cell in the Tower was very small and dark and cold. No fire was ever lit in the tiny fireplace. There was no glass in the two windows, which were barely wider than a man's hand. The only furniture was a chair, a table, and a hard little bed.

The lieutenant of the Tower was an old friend of the More family. He apologized to Thomas for not being allowed to make him more comfortable.

"I'd gladly give you a better cell, and food, and bedding too, but I dare not", he explained. "The king would be extremely angry if I did you any sort of favor."

"Well, I've got nothing to grumble about. If ever I do grumble, just throw me out!" laughed Thomas. Even in prison he could still keep his sense of humor.

Thomas knew it would be stupid to suffer more than he had to, so he made the cell as pleasant as possible. He got permission to have some books brought from home. He blocked out the worst drafts with straw mats, fastening them against the walls and door, as well as putting them on the floor.

The prison food was very bad, but Thomas had never worried about what he ate. Most of the delicacies that kind friends sent in for him Thomas gave to his servant. In those days it was the custom for a gentleman prisoner to have his own servant look after him while he was in jail.

Thomas had a companion in the Tower. Old Bishop Fisher had also been imprisoned for refusing to cooperate with Henry VIII's wicked schemes. The two friends were not allowed to meet, but they sent notes through their servants. They also got great pleasure out of exchanging little gifts of food—a baked custard, a leg of chicken, or a few ripe plums.

While Thomas was settling down in the Tower, Margaret Roper was trying hard to get permission to visit him. At last she succeeded. Thomas was delighted to see her again.

"Darling Meg, how wonderful!" he cried. "Come, let's kneel down and thank God for bringing you to me."

After they had prayed together, they chatted eagerly. Margaret admitted how much she longed for Thomas to be home again.

"So I may be, dearest, if it's God's will", Thomas replied. "I miss you, too. But we're united in our prayers, remember. That's something no amount of separation can take away from us. And you mustn't be sad, because I certainly am not!" Thomas smiled very sweetly. "You know, Meg, the king's councilors are quite wrong if they think it's a punishment for me to be locked up here! But for my wife and you dear children, I'd have become a monk long ago and shut myself away in a cell no better than this. It's so peaceful here; God seems very close. I feel as though he had me on his lap, playing with me!"

Thomas' courage and cheerfulness were amazing. He was often hungry and cold. As his health grew worse, he was often in pain. He was always desperately lonely for his family. Yet he never became depressed because, in his wonderfully adaptable way, he was making the best of his time in jail.

Thomas had spent all his life looking after other people. Now, at last, he had no more responsibilities, and he was free to give all his time to prayer, meditation, and writing. Some of Thomas' most beautiful poems were written during this period in the Tower of London, when he grew closer than ever to God.

Margaret was Thomas' regular visitor, but sometimes

Dame Alice was allowed in to see him. Poor Dame Alice was almost crazy with worry, and she spent most of her visits scolding Thomas. She simply could not understand why Thomas did not give in to the king and agree to the Act of Succession. He would be set free, she reminded him. He would be able to return to Chelsea, where he had everything he could possibly want. Thomas answered quietly that a few years in Chelsea would not be much of an exchange for eternal happiness in heaven.

All the members of Thomas' family were beginning to feel as Dame Alice did. They admired Thomas' perfect trust in God, but they could not quite share it. Through the whole of England people were signing their oaths to the Act of Succession, and the Mores dreaded to think what would happen if Thomas went on refusing. They urged him to sign the oath, and Thomas had a hard time fighting against them. When his beloved Margaret sided with the rest, he was very distressed. He begged her never to come tempting him again, like Eve tempting Adam with the fruit of the forbidden tree. Then Margaret gave him some bad news.

"You told me once, Father, that the king had no right to put you in prison because you hadn't broken any law. Well, Parliament is meeting again, and we hear that a special law is to be passed. It will mean that you and Bishop Fisher are legal prisoners and can be tried and punished."

"I wonder what they'll accuse us of?" said Thomas grimly. "I was afraid this would happen, Meg. I've lain awake for nights on end, wondering what crime they'd say I had committed. Still, I expect King Henry's councilors will think up something!"

"Oh, Father!" wailed Margaret. "I do hope you won't change your mind about the oath when it's too late!"

"On the contrary, I pray God it *will* be too late! I know if ever I were so frightened that I did change my mind, it wouldn't be for the good of my soul!" answered Thomas. Very tenderly he took Margaret in his arms. "Don't worry, Meg. I'm sure God will give me the strength I need. If ever my fear seems too great, I'll cry out to God, like Saint Peter when he was walking on the waters and he began to sink. Then God will put his hand under me and keep me from drowning. God will never let me be lost except through my own fault. And, if the worst happens to me, dearest, pray for me, but don't worry. I shall pray for us, too, that we may all meet again and be merry together in heaven and never have any more trouble."

Thomas' wonderful attitude helped Margaret a great deal. She took courage from him and stopped trying to make him change his mind about the oath.

Summer and autumn passed. New Year's came, and, because Thomas had nothing better to give Bishop Fisher for a present, he sent him a piece of paper with the words "one thousand pounds" written on it in gold letters.

As time went by, Thomas' life in prison became harder. He was not allowed to walk in the Tower garden any more. His papers and pens were taken away from him, so that he had to write with sticks of burned wood on any tiny scraps of paper he could get.

Early in 1535, the new act of Parliament became law. Anyone who openly denied that the king was supreme head of the Church in England would be guilty of high treason. In the sixteenth century, the punishment for high treason was unbelievably cruel. The convicted person was put to death by slow and horrible torture. This was the fate that Henry VIII planned for Bishop John Fisher and Sir Thomas More and anyone else who defied him.

One spring morning in 1535, the king's councilors arrived at the Tower to interview Thomas. They noticed a great change in him. He looked old and very ill, but he refused to sit down while he was being questioned.

"Mr. More, His Grace, the king, wants to know your opinion of his title as head of the Church of England", said Cromwell, the king's secretary.

"Sir, I had hoped King Henry would never ask me that!" Thomas replied. "I don't intend to argue about anybody's title. I'm the king's loyal subject. I pray for him daily and for everyone in the country. But I won't have anything more to do with state matters."

"There's no need to be afraid!" said Cromwell cunningly. "His Grace only wants to be able to set you free and see you about in the world again."

"I've done with the world, and I don't want it given back to me!" Thomas declared. "All I'm concerned with now is to study Christ's Passion and prepare myself to leave this world."

It was obvious that, though Thomas had grown so frail, he was as determined as ever. The councilors sent him away while they consulted together. Then he was called again.

"Mr. More, you're making His Grace very impatient!" said Cromwell sternly. "This obstinate attitude of yours is turning other men against the king."

"I can't help that. I've never given anyone advice, one way or another", Thomas replied. "I've done nobody any harm. I don't think or say anything harmful. In fact, I wish everyone well. And if this isn't enough to keep a man alive, I've no desire to live! As a matter of fact, I'm dying already. Several times lately I've thought I would be gone within an hour, and thank God I've never re-gretted it! On the contrary, I felt sorry when the attack passed off and I knew I wasn't going to die. Well, my body is the king's to do with what he wants. I wish my death might do him good!"

The councilors' hard hearts were softened by this sincere pathetic speech. Thomas was dismissed quite kindly.

A few days later, Margaret was allowed to see Thomas again. They were standing by one of the narrow cell windows when they saw a most horrifying sight.

Four Carthusian monks from the London Charter-house were walking slowly along the path outside. Their hands were tied, and they were surrounded by jailers.

They were on their way to be tortured and put to death
for refusing to recognize Henry VIII as supreme head of
the Church in England. They were the first men to be
martyred by the wicked king. Yet their faces were
wonderfully calm, almost happy.

"Look, Meg!" Thomas exclaimed. "Those good fa-
thers are going to their deaths as cheerfully as bride-
grooms to their marriages! So you see, my dear, the great
difference between people who have devoted their lives
to prayer and penance and people like me who have
wasted their time on worldly things. God knows that
these saintly men have suffered enough, and he is taking
them to himself. But as for me, God knows I'm unworthy, so he leaves me here in the world with all its
unhappiness and trouble!"

"Father, you sound quite envious!" said Margaret in
amazement. "Aren't you frightened to die?"

"Yes, indeed!" Thomas smiled faintly. "I'm a very
great coward, Meg. I'm terrified that I might give way
under torture. But, with God's grace, I'll be able to
endure what he gives me to endure. And then what a
tremendous reward—to be with him forever!"

Thomas longed desperately to be with God. But he
needed every scrap of energy and will power to stand the
strain of waiting, wondering, and being questioned again
and again by the king's councilors.

Bishop Fisher was also being questioned. It was a great
comfort to both Thomas and the bishop knowing that
the other was nearby and sharing the same sort of trouble.

But one day the authorities found out that they had been in touch with each other. Three officials were sent to Thomas' cell with instructions to confiscate his books so that he should have no more paper on which to write messages.

The most important of these officials was a Mr. Rich, a mean, lying character who would do anything to keep in favor with the king. Even charitable Thomas had never been able to like him.

"I'm sorry we must take your books, my friend, but orders are orders", began Mr. Rich smoothly. "Now, while these other two gentlemen are tying the books into bundles, let's have a little private chat. Just between ourselves, do *you* believe His Grace has the right to make himself head of the Church in England? I can't quite make up my mind, so please advise me."

"You must form your own opinions, Mr. Rich", said Thomas. He knew this was a stupid trick to make him give himself away.

"Oh, come, Mr. More! It won't go any farther than these four walls!" lied Mr. Rich.

"I've nothing to say", Thomas answered, turning his back on Mr. Rich.

When the three officials had gone off with the heavy sacks of books, Thomas looked sadly around his bare cell. His books had been his closest companions during many months in jail. Now he had only himself and God. Thomas closed the window shutters and knelt down to pray.

"Gracious me, Mr. More!" exclaimed the Tower lieutenant, entering suddenly. "Whatever are you doing in the dark with the shutters drawn?"

"They've taken my books. My goods are sold, so I might as well shut up shop!" smiled Thomas. The truth was that he realized the time had come for him to concentrate even more on his preparations for death.

The next ten days Thomas spent almost continuously on his knees, praying for his friend Bishop Fisher, as well as for himself.

On June 17, 1535, Bishop Fisher was tried and convicted of high treason. He was to be tortured to death in the usual horrible way. Later, however, Henry VIII decided that the bishop should simply have his head cut off. Thomas said many prayers of thanks when he heard that the king had been a little merciful to the courageous old man.

Bishop Fisher was executed on June 22. Thomas felt very much alone in the world. But he rejoiced with his whole heart because he knew that his friend's suffering had at last come to an end.

11

THE KING'S LOYAL SERVANT—
BUT GOD'S FIRST

ON JULY 1, Thomas left the Tower for the first time in fifteen months. He was being taken upriver to Westminster Hall for his trial.

Many noblemen and officials were waiting in the great hall. They hardly recognized Thomas when he entered, leaning heavily on a stick. The beard he had grown in prison was quite white. His face, once so full of smiles, was as lined as a walnut shell. However, the members of the tribunal were not there to feel sorry for him. The charges against him were read out, and the trial began.

Thomas was accused of three things. He had tried to prevent the king's marriage with Anne Boleyn. He had schemed with Bishop Fisher against Henry VIII. During his conversation in the Tower with Mr. Rich, he had openly denied Henry's right to call himself supreme head of the Church in England.

"You are charged with high treason, Mr. More", said the judge, the lord chancellor himself. "But even now His Grace, the king, might forgive you if you'll stop being obstinate."

"Thank you, my lord. But I pray God I may keep to my true opinions as long as I live", Thomas replied. Now that the many months of waiting were over he felt quite calm. But he knew that he had barely enough strength to last him through a long and difficult trial. When a chair was brought he agreed for once to sit down. Then he began his defense.

"First, my lords, I never tried to prevent the king's second marriage. I just told him my frank opinion, as it was my duty to do. As to maliciously denying His Grace's right to call himself supreme head of the Church in England, your lordships know very well that I've always kept silent about that."

"And by keeping silent you've shown you were against the king!" cried a councilor angrily.

"On the contrary! Silence usually means consent",

replied Thomas with a little smile. "My lords, in cases like this each person must be allowed to follow his own conscience. So long as he doesn't try to influence anyone else, he's guilty of nothing. And, I assure you, I've never discussed the matter with a soul!"

There were no more interruptions, so Thomas went on to prove that he had never schemed with Bishop Fisher.

"You say, my lords, that the bishop and I made exactly the same answers when we were questioned in the Tower", he finished. "Well, since we've had the same type of education and think very much in the same way, isn't it natural we'd speak alike?"

There was silence in the great hall. No one could deny anything that Thomas had said, and for a moment it seemed that he must win his case. But the tribunal was made up of crafty men, and they were determined to convict him of treason. Mr. Rich was called and began to give evidence.

"My lords, on the afternoon of June 12, I had the following conversation with the prisoner in his cell. 'Mr. More,' I said, 'you're a wise man, so tell me this. If Parliament declared me to be king, wouldn't you agree that I was king?' 'Certainly', replied Mr. More. 'But, Mr. Rich, if Parliament declared that God wasn't God, would you agree?' 'Of course not', I said. 'Parliament can't make such laws.' 'Neither can Parliament make the king supreme head of the Church!' said Mr. More. Then I knew, my lords, that he was an evil traitor!"

The members of the tribunal exchanged triumphant glances. The lord chancellor looked at Thomas.

"Well, Mr. More? Have you anything to say?"

"Yes, indeed, my lord!" cried Thomas, who had turned white with indignation and horror. He swung around to face the lying witness. "Mr. Rich, if what you've said is true, then I pray that I may never see God! Indeed, I'm sorrier for your lie than for my own danger at this moment! I've known you for years, and I've never once confided in you. Nor has anyone else that I know of. I'm sorry you make me say this, but you've always had an evil reputation as a gambler and a gossiper. Therefore, my lords, does it seem likely that I'd discuss with Mr. Rich an important matter which I've always refused to discuss with the king himself, or with the king's honorable councilors? Can you really believe this to be possible?"

"But I've got witnesses!" shouted Mr. Rich, looking around for the two men who had been with him in Thomas' cell that afternoon.

However, when the point came, these men felt too ashamed to agree with Mr. Rich's lies. They said feebly that they had been too busy packing up Sir Thomas' books to hear the conversation.

There was no more evidence to be heard. Now everything depended on the members of the jury. They must have known quite well that Thomas was innocent, but they also knew what verdict Henry VIII expected them to bring in. They left the hall to discuss the case. For fifteen minutes Thomas prayed silently for strength. Then the jury returned.

"Well? What's your verdict?" asked the lord chancellor. The foreman stood stiffly at attention.

"Guilty, my lord."

The lord chancellor nodded and at once began to declare sentence on Thomas. But Thomas interrupted. There was no longer any hope for him, yet he showed no sign of his fear as he spoke.

"My lord, when I practiced law it was usual before passing sentence to ask the prisoner if he had anything to say."

"Very well", growled the chancellor. He was a weak character, but not evil, and he was not enjoying this trial. "Have you anything to say, Mr. More?"

"Yes, my lord," said Thomas.

Then at last he ended his years of discreet silence and boldly condemned Henry VIII for declaring himself head of the Church in England. When he had finished, he sat back in his chair and listened quietly as the death sentence was read out.

"He shall be drawn on a hurdle through the city of London to Tyburn", recited the lord chancellor formally. "There he shall be hanged till he is half dead, then cut down, his stomach cut open, his intestines burned, and his four limbs set up over the four gates of the city, his head upon London Bridge."

Thomas had a vivid imagination. He realized the terrible sufferings he must face. Yet he spoke in a clear, firm voice when he was asked for the last time if he had anything to say.

"Just this, my lords. In the Acts of the Apostles we read how Saint Paul consented to, and was present at, the stoning to death of Saint Stephen. Now they are together in heaven. So I pray, my lords, that though you've been my judges here on earth, we, too, may meet in heaven to our everlasting salvation."

The trial was over. Wearily Thomas set out with his jailers for the journey downriver, back to the Tower. The people of London had already heard that their friend Sir Thomas was to die. A huge crowd was waiting at the Tower wharf. John More, Margaret Roper, and Margaret Clement were there also, standing in a tragic little group.

As soon as Margaret Roper caught sight of her dear father, she pushed through the rough crowds, past the prison guards with their great spears, and flung her arms around Thomas' neck.

"Oh, my father! Oh, my father!" she sobbed.

"Don't upset yourself, Margaret. It's the will of God", he murmured lovingly and did his best to soothe her. The guards pulled her away and walked on with Thomas. But Margaret came running after them. She was weeping bitterly, and Thomas himself was very near tears as they hugged each other for the last time.

"Dearest Meg, pray for me!" he whispered. Then the guards separated them. He never saw Margaret again.

Back in his little cell, Thomas had a few more days for

prayer and meditation. He was told that Henry VIII had ordered his sentence to be changed. He was to be executed instead of tortured to death. He felt tremendously thankful, and, now that he had nothing to fear, he began to look forward eagerly to death.

On July 5, Thomas made his final preparations. He collected together his coarse hair shirt, a handkerchief, and other small belongings that he knew his family would want to have as keepsakes of him. Then he wrote his last letter to Margaret.

This little note was full of tenderness and unselfish thoughts for his dear ones. It contained the sort of practical instructions that any man might write down for a trusted eldest daughter before setting out on a journey, leaving at home relatives and servants who must be cared for after he had gone.

When exactly he would have to go Thomas did not know. But he told Margaret that he hoped it would be the following day, July 6, the octave of the feast of those two great martyrs, Saints Peter and Paul. Thomas felt it would be a very suitable day for him to go to God.

Thomas' wish was granted. Early next morning an old friend came to break the news that Thomas was to die before nine o'clock.

Thomas' first thought was for his family. He felt very happy when he heard that the king had given permission for them to attend his burial.

"I owe His Grace much for all the favors he has done me", he remarked sincerely. "I'm particularly grateful to

King Henry for having had me shut up here all these months. It's given me a chance to prepare myself for death."

Thomas' friend was so touched by this wonderful forgiveness and humility that he broke down completely. Instead of his friend comforting Thomas, it was Thomas, the doomed man, who had to comfort him. Afterward Thomas began to get ready for his execution.

In those days it was the custom for the executioner to receive his victim's clothes as a part of his payment. Unselfish Thomas wanted to give his executioner something worthwhile, so he changed into an expensive silk robe that a friend had sent him. The lieutenant of the Tower had great difficulty persuading him to change back into his rough prison clothes.

"Think how your wife or daughters would appreciate such a lovely robe!" he urged. "Don't waste it on a common executioner!"

"Oh, very well, if you insist", laughed Thomas. "But I'd like my executioner to have a good reward. I've still got a few gold pieces, so please give him one of those."

"As you wish, Mr. More", agreed the lieutenant. He was amazed that any man could be so thoughtful and so calm as he prepared to die.

Thomas finished dressing. The guards came, and he was taken out of the dark Tower into the dazzling summer sunshine.

The whole of London seemed to be waiting outside for him. Some of the crowd were weeping; some jeered at him. Thomas offered up his ordeal to God and stepped out bravely. But he was very weak. His pace became slower and slower. A kind woman pushed past the guards and held out a mug of wine. Thomas shook his head.

"Jesus Christ was given bitter gall, not wine", he reminded her. Another woman called angrily to him.

"Mr. More! Do you remember me? When you were lord chancellor you passed wrong judgment against me in court!"

"Madam, I remember you well", said Thomas wearily. "And, if I were judging your case again, I shouldn't alter my verdict against you! No wrong has been done you, so be satisfied and leave me alone."

The next person to draw Thomas' attention was a man who, for years, had worried himself almost out of his mind. Thomas had helped this man before, and now he begged Thomas to help him again. Thomas looked pityingly at him and told him to go in peace. As if by a miracle the man was completely cured of his mental troubles.

At last, Thomas arrived at the scaffold. He was full of joy because the moment had come for him to leave the cares of the world behind. But he did not have the strength to climb the scaffold steps alone. He asked to be helped and made a little joke to encourage the prison officials. Then he looked down at the crowd around the scaffold.

"Pray for me in this world, citizens of London, and I shall pray for you in the next", he said. "I beg all of you to pray for our king, too, that God may guide him. I am dying for our Catholic faith, good people. And I call you to witness that I die the king's loyal servant—but God's first."

Thomas knelt down and said an act of contrition. Then the executioner came forward and asked Thomas' forgiveness for having to cut off his head. Thomas kissed him warmly.

"You're going to do me a great favor today!" he said. "Cheer up, man, and don't mind doing your job. My neck is very short, so see you aim straight. You don't want to spoil your reputation!"

Thomas turned to smile good-bye to the lieutenant of the Tower, who was weeping openly. He bound his eyes with a handkerchief that the executioner held out to him. He was still humbly begging God's mercy as he knelt down and put his head on the wooden execution block. The executioner swung his axe.

"Stop!" cried Thomas suddenly. "I must put my beard aside. It would be a shame to chop it off. After all, my poor beard is not accused of treason!"

That was Thomas' last joke. A second later the axe fell, and a great sigh went up from the spectators. Thomas More lay dead.

That last hour had shown Thomas as he had been during the whole of his wonderful life. He had considered everyone but himself. He had been loyal to his king without feeling any bitterness for the terrible way Henry VIII had treated him. He had been full of humor, so that even during the grimmest moments laughter was not far off. Most important of all, he had never forgotten for a second that a man's life and suffering are only a short preparation for the everlasting happiness of heaven. In his own words, Thomas More had been the king's loyal servant—but God's first.

Author's Note

There can be few saints more rewarding than Saint Thomas More for what they have left of themselves by their own writings. In the preparation of this book I have found particularly useful Ralph Robinson's translation of *Utopia* and the selection from Thomas More's works made by P. S. and H. M. Allen. Another scholar to whom I am indebted is E. V. Hitchcock for her edition of that unique record, *Life of More*, by his son-in-law William Roper.

I should like to make acknowledgment for Father T. E. Bridgett's *Life and Writings of Thomas More* and for *Saint Thomas More* by E. E. Reynolds. Of the biographies by non-Catholic writers to which I have referred, *Sir Thomas More and His Friends* by E. M. G. Routh has been most illuminating in its wealth of personal detail. Above all, however, my thanks are due to R. W. Chambers for his *Thomas More*, an incomparable biography that has been my chief source of information.

Other works for which I have been grateful are *Wolsey* by A. F. Pollard, *Political History of England (1485–1547)* by H. A. L. Fisher, and *English Social History* by G. M. Trevelyan.

Lastly, I should like to express sincere thanks to Father Alfonso de Zulueta for his kind interest and advice on the choice of literature and to Miss Christine Campbell Thomson for her unfailing encouragement.

All of the material in this book has been collected from the most authoritative sources, and, though the work has been dramatized to make it more appealing to its young audience, every incident is based upon historical fact.